Dreaming of You

By Minniel Douglas

Dedication

This book is dedicated to everyone on the journey of finding divine vision for their lives. Divine Vision has an appointed manifestation date. Rushing the process is not an option. Trust the Creator. Peace, Beloved.

Thank you to my wonderful family (my husband, my kids, my Mommie) for all of your love, support, and patience as I write. Thank you to everyone who allowed me to ask questions about your life visions and your process of walking in divine vision. Your honesty and transparency truly helped me along the way. And last but not least, thank you, God, for this gift and for choosing to use me to write such an extraordinary story.

I love you all forever and always.

Copyright

Note:

This title is for adults only. It contains some themes, actions, and language that may be offensive to some.

Contents

Part 1: Choices

Chapter 1 - LeShay

"Trust me." He says as he takes my hand, kisses the back of it, and then the palm. He leads me to a park where kids are playing on the playground. They slide down the slides and swing on the swings. They laugh and enjoy themselves as they run here and there, and there we are, holding hands and watching them. He squeezes my hand and begins to walk again.

This time, he leads me through a neighborhood filled with beautiful stucco and stone houses. The houses are various shades of brown and gray with specially colored doors. As we walk, we eventually reach a home with a purple door and a glittery finish. He walks us up the walkway, and then he presses the door code. He leads me into the high-ceilinged foyer with a crystal chandelier. The sun shines on the chandelier just right, causing the crystals to give off beautiful, bright-colored lights in an array of colors. He waits patiently for me to take in everything the house has to offer. He allows me the time to examine the colors of the walls, the unique paintings hanging in strategic places, and the blue-gray furniture and large windows.

After some time, he takes me to the primary bedroom and sits me on the chaise in front of the bay window without allowing me the pleasure of viewing the backyard. As I look around the room, I notice there is no bed in the room. There is only artwork, as if the owner of the house wanted to have their own private art gallery. He pulls the shades and closes the blackout curtains, leaving us in darkness until he switches on the paintings' spotlights. Then, he removes the coverings from the canvases lining the walls, one by one. With each painting revealed, I see myself as I grow from a baby to a girl to a young woman to a woman. When he gets to the last painting, there is nothing on the canvas. It's just white.

It is then that I finally look up at this man who has been leading me all this time. I know who he is before I look into his face. As I gaze over his face, my eyes eventually meet the eyes of the man I have known since college. The eyes of the man whom I gave my heart to one day on the yard. The eyes of the man who is my peace, my protector, my love, and my best friend. Those dark brown eyes tell me stories of what is and what is to come.

After a moment, he turns from me and picks up a paintbrush from a table that has appeared out of nowhere. He begins to paint a new picture. One that starts with the purple door with a glittery finish. Suddenly, he stops, looks back at me, and says, "I need you." I must look confused because he repeats himself a little louder than before. "I need you. Wake up. Now!"

I wake up instantly and find myself breathing hard and sitting up quickly. I clutch my chest and take slow, deep breaths. After a few minutes, my breathing has regulated, and I can think a little more clearly. I used to have realistic dreams like these all the time. It was like the Divine always waited for me to sleep to start explaining the details of my life. But as things got busy with my career and my life, I stopped dreaming as much. The Divine and I talk every morning, but that is it. No dreams.

I begin to think about the dream. The man in my dream is my best friend, Monroe Marquis Thibodeaux. He is a general surgeon in the shock/trauma department at one of the prestigious hospitals here in Houston, and he works damn hard.

As these thoughts go through my mind, I remember what he said in the dream. *"I need you. Wake up. Now!"* I look at my clock, and it is 3:00am, which means he is probably asleep or in the OR. But my spirit is saying, "Call him, NOW." Immediately, I pick up my cell phone and select his name from my favorites. It rings once, and he picks it up.

"Hey……" He says extremely slowly and slurred.

"Roe?" I ask cautiously. My best friend is not the type to be drunk, and definitely not the kind to be drunk in the middle of the night on a Tuesday. I remove my sheet, move to the edge of my bed, and let my feet hang off the side of the bed.

"Yeah……" He says again, just as slowly and just as slurred. I hear smooth R&B playing in the background.

"Baby, where are you? Are you ok?"

"Probably not" is the response he gives me.

"What does that mean? Where are you?" I question a little more urgently. I get up, pull out one of my jogging sets, and begin to dress as I wait for him to reply. Something is definitely wrong.

"Just out..."

I am beyond worried at this point. What is it with these slow, slurred, short sentences? "Baby, are you drunk?" I ask him.

"No..."

"Then, what?" I deadpan him.

"I may have done something else or mixed a few things."

What in the entire Hell!! This boy doesn't do drugs. What is he talking about? At this point, I am heading down the stairs to grab my keys. "Monroe, where are you?" I ask sternly.

"At Da Spot."

"Da Spot?... Monroe, for real, where are you?" I ask him again because the Da Spot is a place we used to hang out in New Orleans when I was in college and he was in medical school. So, he definitely can not be there.

"For real. I am..." He shuffles around like he is changing positions. I hear a lady's sultry voice asking him if he wants some more or if he would like to try something else. I listen to him say, "Nah, thank you for now." Then, he returns to me and says, "Babe, I'm at the Da Spot."

"Monroe, tell that woman to get you a coffee, and I am calling Cristo to come get you. I will see you in a few hours. Do you hear me?"

"Don't call Cristo." He pleads. His voice is deep and smooth when he says, "I know I sound bad. No, Cristo. Please."

"Fine. I'll call Marcus. Stay put, and have coffee. Ok?"

"Ok."

With that, we hang up, and I call Roe's brother, Marcus.

"Gurl, you better have a good reason to be calling me at this time of the night...No, Baby. Go back to sleep. It is just LeShay." I can hear his wife respond, "It better be."

"Sorry, Marcus, but I need your help. Roe is at the Da Spot. He is either drunk or on something. Can you please go get him?"

Laughing, he says, "Gurl, there is no way my brother is either of those things. Plus, how is he here anyway?"

"Marcus, I am serious. I have never heard him this way, and I don't know how he is in New Orleans. Will you go, please? Just take him to his hotel or wherever he is staying and text me the address. When do you leave again?"

"Tomorrow...well, today at 9am. I can bring him here, but the wife has to go to work." I hear him getting dressed as he is talking.

"No, just take him wherever he is staying. I will be there in 5 hours."

"Shay, don't get no tickets."

"I got this. You good?"

"Yeah, I'm headed to the Da Spot. I'll text you."

Chapter 2 – LeShay

As I am driving down I-10 E, my nerves are shot. Monroe is the reasonable one in our duo. He is the one who follows the rules and pays attention to details. He is the one you call in the middle of the night to come get you, not you needing to go get him. I have never heard him so not just intoxicated, but not together. Even when he drinks, there is a method to his madness. He is always in control. In fact, that is how I met him.

I was at Da Spot with my gurls. We had just finished midterms and were out trying to have a good time. "Trying" being the operative word because one of my gurls, Carmen, was crying over her ex-boyfriend, yet again. As we walked into the lounge, she saw said ex-boyfriend all up in some girl's face with his hands roaming her body as they were grinding to the music. Carmen first got mad, but after three drinks, she was crying her eyes out about him being the love of her life and yada yada yada. That boy was not the love of her life or the man of her dreams. She hyped him up in her mind since the break-up, like always. This was something my other friend, Sena, was in the middle of telling her. As they went back and forth about the situation, I decided to get another drink and go stand on the balcony outside. What I loved about Da Spot was that it was in the French Quarter overlooking Jackson Square. Yes, I loved Bourbon Street, like everyone else, but sometimes you need a place to sit, chill, and vibe while having a good time. And that place was the Da Spot. It had good music, good food, and great drinks.

I went outside onto the balcony and sat on one of the lounge chairs. Watching the moon always seemed to calm my nerves and make me reflective. So as I sat drinking my Jack and Coke, I thought about my dream the night before. It was about a man. He was lying in the grass at the park and covered in roses. When I walked up to him, well up on him, he smiled and said, "Hi, Gorgeous. I found you. He said you would come." Then, I woke up. I could not remember the man's face when I awoke, but I could remember his presence and his energy. It was like I could feel him with me. It was the weirdest thing.

As I sat on the balcony, I allowed that feeling to surround me. In fact, it seemed to get more intense the longer I thought about it. Then, I heard the man's voice again from somewhere behind me. It was deep and raspy, kind of like an after-dark R&B radio show host. I turned in the direction of the voice because, certainly, I was tripping. But then, I heard it again, and there he was, the guy the voice belonged to.

He was on the phone. He was talking about his mother or something. I wasn't really listening; I was mesmerized by the voice, his voice. I felt the urge to approach him, but how could I? I did not know this man, and just because his voice was similar to the man in my dream, what did that matter? Then, the guy looked my way, and my heart stopped beating. The eyes that met mine were the same dark brown eyes from my dream. They were confident, assured, and loving. They saw me, and I saw them. I heard him tell whoever he was on the phone with that he would call them back. Then, he walked over to me, sat in the lounge chair across from mine, and we just stared at each other. Until he finally said, "Hi, Gorgeous."

"Hi," I replied with a smile.

"This is going to sound weird, and I promise I am not crazy…..Um, I saw you in my dreams last night." He paused and waited for my response. Before I could respond, a group of guys came outside.

"Roe, there you are. You still calculated tipsy, or have you realized drunk is where it's at?" One of them yelled our way.

The guy whom I now knew as Roe smirked slightly and, while still staring at me, said over his shoulder, "Calculated tipsy is a thing and works quite well." His friends looked past him at me, and they all smiled and waved in my direction. I waved back. I mean, why not? Then one of the guys said, "We gone catch you later."

"Sounds like a plan," Roe replied while still making eye contact with me. His friends left, and he arched an eyebrow at me as if to say *Your turn.*

I started with, "So, Roe, is it?"

"Monroe, to be exact, but Roe is cool too."

"You said you dreamt about me?"

His voice dropped an octave. It seemed natural, like it was a reflex, not like he was trying to hit on me, but it sounded amazing all the same. "Yeah...crazy, huh?"

I smirked, "A little...But I dreamt about you, too."

"Last night?" His voice rose in excitement.

"Yeah..." I smiled.

Of course, it was then that my gurls decided to come outside. But unlike his friends, they were ready to go to stop number two, and I had to go. You know the rule: we came together, so we leave together. I hated that rule so much at that moment.

"Sorry, I have to go," I told him.

He turned and looked at my friends. Then, he looked back at me. "I get the distinct feeling that you and I should stay in contact. So, do you mind if we exchange numbers?"

"I would love to," I say, handing him my phone as he hands me his. "The name is LeShay, by the way," I said after returning his phone.

He smiled beautifully and nodded in appreciation. As he looked at my name in his phone, he sent me a text, which made my phone ping. I looked at it and laughed. I sent him a text back as I stood up.

He smiled and said, "Just checking." I smiled and waved bye-bye. Then my friends and I left, and nothing in my life was ever the same again.

That memory always warms my heart. It reminds me that Roe and I are meant to be connected in this life. I just have never been able to figure out what kind of connection and how deeply. As this thought is rattling through my brain, I get a text from Marcus letting me know they are at the W Hotel on Chartres St. That kind of makes sense since it is Monroe's favorite hotel chain, but in New Orleans he usually stays at the Marriot on Canal St. so he can people watch. Interesting. I text Marcus, thanking him and letting him know I will be there in a couple of hours. Marcus agrees to stay with Roe until he has to leave, which gives me a little relief.

I arrive at the W Hotel two hours and some change after our call, with Marcus leaving about 45 minutes before my arrival. I walked through the modern and soothing lobby design and asked the reservationist for the package that Marcus left for me. Inside the package is the key to Roe's 3rd-floor room and some more of Marcus's special herbal hangover pills. I use the key to access the 3rd floor and try my best to calm down as the elevator takes me up. I stroll to Roe's room, taking intentional breaths in an effort to reach that place of peace that will ensure that I do not escalate whatever is going on with him.

I am utterly flabbergasted when I walk into the room, so much for being calm and peaceful. Looking around the room in more detail, there are paintings on easels everywhere, there is paint on the counter, there are different color jars of paint open and not being used, and brushes are in cups all along the counter, like he could not be bothered to rinse them out.

Understand that Roe's hobby is painting, and he is exceptionally good at it. However, this place is nowhere near as neat and organized as Roe's art room in his house. His art room at home is clean all the time. This room is a mess.

I walk up to the first painting, and it looks like the back of his dream house that he is currently building. I have only seen that portion of the house in pictures, as he will not let me visit just yet. Anyway, I walk up to the next painting, and there is a woman with no face and kids without faces playing in the front yard of a blurred-out house. The next easel holds a canvas that is painted all black, like he needs to come back to it. Then, the last easel causes me to stop breathing. It is a house with a purple door, but not just any purple door. It is royal purple with hints of silver shimmer, just like in my dream. The painting is a close-up of the door, so you cannot see the rest of the front of the house, but that is the door. My door.

I hear what I assume is the bathroom door opening behind me, but I cannot take my eyes off the painting. *God, what in the world?* I pray silently. As soon as Monroe walks out of the bathroom, I feel it; this instantaneous shift of the energy in the room. It is the same feeling as the first time I dreamt about him. His energy is warm, inviting, confident, and soothing. It presses into me, passing by outer defenses and right to the heart of me.

His energy is usually laced with peace and calm that is sturdy and unwavering, but today, something is different. The peace is not there. I wait for him to approach me. I assess his energy some more as I continue to stare at the purple door painting. When he reaches me, he wraps his arms around my waist and rests his cheek against my ear.

As I let my hands rest on his, he kisses the space right in front of my ear, then whispers, "I know."

I turn in his arms with a knitted brow. I ask, "Know what?"

"I know you dreamt about me. That is why you called me. I know you probably dreamt about this door too because I have been dreaming about it for months, and last night I had had enough." His voice is steady, but again, the peace is gone. What is happening here? Whatever had him intoxicated earlier has cleared his system, probably thanks to Marcus and his antidotes for hangovers and getting high, such as the pills currently in my purse by the door.

I don't understand the feeling I am getting off of him. I search his eyes, but he stops my assessment by looking over my head and bringing me into his chest. This is easy to do as he is 6'1" and I am 5'5". I can hear the steady beat of his heart. I take a deep breath before asking, "Monroe, Baby, tell me what is going on......Please."

"Kira wants me to propose to her." He states as he steps back and takes a seat on the couch. His suite is made of an array of greens and oranges, and has a living space, a desk, and two doors. Interesting on many levels.

He pulls me onto his lap. Then, he places me on the couch and slowly maneuvers our bodies so that his head is on my chest. The rest of his body is lying to the side of me, and I am now cuddling his head into me. His face is pointed up toward my face, so I see his features and facial expressions. But, still, he keeps his averted so that I cannot read the depths of his heart and soul.

Typically, we take this position with his eyes gazing into mine when we are about to discuss something heavy on his heart. But today, he does not want me to read to him; he wants to talk, that much I can tell. So, I wait for him to continue.

"I told her I couldn't. She yelled and screamed about how I had been wasting her time. She asked me when I thought I would be ready..." He breathed heavily and shook his head. "For the first time, I decided to be honest. I love her, but I cannot marry her. Something deep within me keeps telling me, 'No.' I have been fighting it. You know this." I nod. Because I do know that he stayed with her because she fit into his world, but there was always something that stopped him from moving forward.

He continues, "That was one month ago."

"I'm sorry, come again?" I ask with irritation and shock, lacing my voice.

"You heard me. Look, I know, but before you get mad." He says as he sits up and makes eye contact with me. "You were at that convention giving that presentation, which changed the game for you. I didn't want to interrupt that. I intended to tell you at our weekly dinner. But things have been crazy."

"Fine, but a month, Babes?" I question, still slightly irritated, because I appreciate the gesture, but seriously.

He smirks at the nickname. "Can I finish?"

I roll my eyes, shake my head, and then say, "Yes" while wearing the same smirk he is wearing.

"She broke up with me. Said I needed to figure out what I wanted. I wanted to argue, but the truth was that she was right. We had been together for four years. I should know what I want. That night, she left; she said she would be back to get her stuff the next day while I was rounding at work.

"Then, that night, the dreams started. I dreamt about the back of the house, then the front of the house, then the front yard, and then the door. What got me the most was that the woman and kids in my dream were mine, but I could not see their faces or sense their energy. It was closed or blocked to me. Then, that purple door kept showing up." He pauses and looks at the painting that is now behind me. He shakes his head, "It just keeps showing up...... Finally, in one of the dreams, I stopped looking at the door and I tried to open it, but I couldn't. It was like it was locked to me, too, just like the woman and kids. Last night, I dreamt about roses covering me, and I felt you come in and stand over me, but I woke up before I could see you. I was drenched in sweat and so confused.... Noted, I had been drinking before I went to sleep. So, when I got up, I decided that if sleep wouldn't give me peace, I was going out. That is how I ended up at the Da Spot popping who knows what."

"I'm sorry, come again? You popped what?"

"You heard me. I don't know. Before you get all, 'You know better,' I know. I just... needed a reprieve. It wasn't working as it is, and your call officially ended my downward spiral, anyway."

"Good, cause you sounded like a mess. I was worried."

His gaze meets mine, "I know...... Sorry. It was reckless. I'm good now. I promise. Marcus came through."

"Umm hmm," I say as I shake my head and look towards my purse with the extra pills inside for just in case. Then, it hits me, "Wait, how long have you been in New Orleans? What about work?"

"Five days, and I took leave."

My concern rises again, "Roe, what's going on?" I ask once more.

"I haven't been able to sleep more than two hours a night since everything with Kira happened. My hands had started to shake sometimes, and my vision had begun to blur...... I can't cut on anyone like this." He states as he looks at his hands. When he looks back at me, he continues, "So, I took my vacation days that I had never used and put in for a three-week leave. I came here hoping that I would find reprieve, but I haven't."

"Why didn't you call me?"

"For what? What can you do, Shay? My gurl left, and I ain't mad; my job is fine; my brain is what…messed up. Can you stop the dreams so that I can sleep? Can you make the purple door open or stop appearing at all so that I can sleep? Can you tell me who that woman in my dreams is, or make my kid's faces appear in my dreams?" He questions me firmly. He gets up and walks to the window, looking over the balcony. With his back still to me, he finally states calmly, "No, you can't. You can't tell me any of that. So, I haven't called. I wasn't ready to talk…. But when I had that dream about the roses, I knew you would come. I wasn't surprised when you called. After all, that is how we work."

I wasn't sure how to take that last statement. It was almost like he was mad that I was here. I waited, but he didn't say anything else, so I stood and asked, "Do you want me to go?" He still did not say anything; he just kept looking outside.

"Monroe, do you want me to leave?" I ask more firmly.

He drops his head and shakes it no. Then, I hear something I have never heard in our ten years of friendship: he's crying. I can hear his soft sobs, and then he places his hands on the glass doors for support. My heart breaks as the man who is my rock is falling apart. I walk to him slowly. When I reach him, I slide my arms around him, embracing him from behind. I rest my head on his back and hold him gently until our breathing syncs. I am sure he is keeping something from me, but I am also sure he does not want to tell me. I don't know what to do. *God help.* I pray silently.

Next thing I know, I am asking Roe one simple question, "What do you need?"

Chapter 3 – Monroe

That should be a simple question, but it's not. How do I tell her what I need when I don't know? I am used to knowing what I need and want. I am usually very clear and strategic about everything. Some people may call me anal or type A but to each their own. I am calculated in the best of ways. It makes me great at my job and observant with those I love. But lately, I find myself at a loss. I know I told Shay about the issue that started a month ago, but the truth is that the problem started about a year ago.

One year ago, I went to this medical conference to gain new insight into the best practices and standards in my field, Trauma Surgery. I attended the conference to learn about new techniques and up-and-coming developments in the industry. My girlfriend, Kira, and I went to the conference because it was in Atlanta, and she wanted to see her friends while I was there. We had a plan. I would go to the conference during the day, and she would hang out with her friends. I was to text her when I was done or if I was going to have a meeting during dinner. If we were both available, we would have a date and hang out in the city.

It was a good plan. The problem was that when we got there, I found out she had not told her friends she was coming. This meant that two of her friends were out of town, and the other one who was left was stuck at home with her new baby. Kira visited her friend with the baby, but that only lasted two days. On day three, Kira decided to stay in the hotel and wait for me.

Yes, it went as badly as it sounds. She called and texted me all day long. By midday on day five, I had had enough and told her she needed to find something to do. Of course, that led to an argument and then to my agreeing to let her splurge on a mini shopping spree so I could work. When I returned to the hotel that evening, Kira had spent over 10k on my credit card. 10k!! What did she think this was? I made her take half of the things she bought back. She pouted and whined the whole flight home.

Once we got back to Houston, things did not fully return to normal. She had this notion that since I was a surgeon, she should be able to buy what she wanted when she wanted. Don't get me wrong. Yes, I get paid well and I/we could buy what we wanted but within reason and strategically. Some things had to be planned for. I did have to finish paying my student loans and all these insurance bills that are required for me to practice in my field, but she was not trying to hear me. Eventually, at dinner nine months ago, we had this conversation.

"Baby, why are you acting like this? It is only a $3,000 purse. You should want to buy it for me." Kira asked sweetly over dinner.

"Don't call me that," I stated plainly as I ate my tasteless food because Kira was on a no-sweets and no-salt diet.

"Why, you are my man? I don't understand why you don't like nicknames. You and LeShay have them. I have heard you all numerous times." She was getting angry.

I looked up slowly and took some nice deep breaths to keep my calm, I stated, *"Leave LeShay out of this. This is about the fact that even though I do not mind buying you a purse for $3,000 or $5,000 on occasions, those occasions are not every week. Money does not grow on trees."*

"You're a surgeon, and we can afford it." She stated so matter fact-ly that I had to look up again. Because truly, who was this woman? Kira and I worked as a couple because she was just as methodical as I was. She understood how to plan and make moves. She understood vision and would follow. What this was, I had no idea, but I did not like it.

"Kira, where is this coming from?" I questioned her as I observed her reactions closely. She started moving and fidgeting in her seat and playing with her hands. She took a long pause, which did not bother me. She knew this, as well. I can do silence. I will wait you out. You will not win that game with me. I continued to eat as I waited. Finally, she breathed dramatically, another new trait that I did not like.

"Look, I have been talking to some trusted advisors, and they said they think I should live a little. I want to be happy and enjoy life and not plan everything all the time. I want to get married and have kids with you. I want to live the luxury life we have always talked about."

"Kira, I have never said I wanted the luxury life."

"Boo-bear, but you do want it. I can tell every time we go to one of your colleagues' parties, and their wives walk

around in expensive shoes and clothes, drinking only the best champagne."

"Who are you talking about? We have only been to Jaheem's party, and he and his wife are in the planning stages of life, too."

"I'm not talking about them. I am talking about your boss and his wife. I met his wife in Atlanta, and we ended up having a great time together. She has been teaching me about being a surgeon's wife. Well, she and her friends have been teaching me."

"Is that who you have been talking to every Saturday at wherever it is that you've been going?"

"It is called hot yoga for the last time." She raised her voice out of frustration. "And yes."

I leaned forward and stared into her eyes. Then, I took a nice, long look at the woman in front of me. I realized at that moment that I had not been really looking at her lately. I had been so busy with extra shifts trying to make money for my house that was about to break ground that I had missed what was happening in the house I live in now.

She looked different. She got her hair cut, that I knew. However, when you looked at her as the whole package, the short haircut with the Versace Pajamas, black toenail polish, red lipstick, and a diamond choker all for dinner at home for two, I realized this woman before was not my Kira at all. What was going on? The woman before me was not my Kira. This woman did not have the same values or vision as I do. She was not the woman I met and fell in love with years ago. This woman was different, and I didn't like it.

"Kira, what is going on?" I asked one last time with restrained anger.

"I WANT LUXURY!" She yelled and then smiled weirdly. She paused and, then, said sweetly, "And you are going to give it to me." She crossed her legs, showing me her upper thigh, and then used her leg to run her foot up the inside of my groin.

I scooted back immediately and then leaned forward as she was sitting next to me at the dinner table while I sat at the head. I steadied my voice and clenched my teeth before I stated calmly, "First, you are out of your got' damn mind if you think you are going to sit here and yell at me like you are my boss's white-washed fake ass, second wife... Second, I am not. Hear me real clear, I am not funding some crazy luxury experiment you are on because you have decided to drink the surgeon's wife Kool-Aid. I am not that dude. I have not been that dude, and no matter how much I make, I will never be that dude. Do not try whatever this is again. Period."

She stared back at me in shock. I had never spoken to her so stern and void of emotion. It was my doctor's voice and presence. The one I get when we are in an emergency surgery and there is no room for questions or stalling, we need to move and move now. With that being said, I stood up from the table and went to take a shower.

The days, weeks, and months following got more tense. Kira was still hanging out with Isabella, my boss's wife and Isabella was still feeding her the same shit. I was irritated with Kira for drinking the Kool-Aid, but a part of me understood. I wanted to sip it too from time to time; but if I was going to achieve what I wanted to achieve, I could not do that, and I needed my woman on the same page with me. As things got tense, I started drinking. I went from social drinking to a drink every night to multiple drinks a night.

About four months ago, I fell asleep in my study, and I started having dreams about houses and neighborhoods. Then, I started dreaming about multiple color doors. There were green ones and red ones and orange ones. Then, I got to the house. I could not see the front of it. The backyard was gorgeous, though. It had a grilling station with an outdoor bar. There was wood flooring on the covered patio which looked out on the huge pool with a nice rock design that encased a slide.

In my dreams, I revisited this house many times, but only the backyard. Every time I revisited this house, more was revealed to me. Eventually, this house became the inspiration for the house I am building now.

Spiritually, I know dreams are not just dreams; they mean things. I have had many occasions where this has been true, like when I met LeShay. But the truth is that with some dreams, you know the meaning is good; with some dreams, you know the meaning is bad; and with some dreams, you are not sure what the meaning will be, if the meaning will be good or bad. The dreams I kept having about this house made me feel like I was not ready for what would be said if I asked the Divine what it meant. But the more I dreamt about this house, the more my relationship with Kira was going down in flames.

There was issue after issue. It went from money to how I dressed to me not having time for her anymore to my drinking to her not knowing me anymore to me needing to choose because she was too amazing to be wasting her time on me if I did not want to marry her. By the time we got to last month, I was stressed, worn out, and frustrated. My peace was gone, and I was spending all my time trying not to ask the question burning in my soul, which was, "What did these dreams mean?"

Right now, in this moment, with Shay waiting on me to answer the question, "What do I need," I can feel her make soothing circles over my heart as she embraces me from behind. Her touch is firm but gentle in a way that only a Reiki Master's touch can be. She does not do Reiki anymore for clients, but I think she misses it. I feel her breathing with me, matching me, and unintentionally becoming one with me in this moment. She is the only person I am okay with truly sharing energy with me in the way she is doing right now. I know she feels my unease.

I don't know how to tell her about the house dreams. I think it's because I know, even though I have not seen inside, that she is the one in that house with the purple door. I know that she is inside. I feel her energy radiating from the house, from the land the house sits on. It took me a few dreams before I realized that what I was feeling coming off the house energetically was her. She felt different though. It was her, but there was this completeness and wholeness that I could not explain.

I still have not answered the question of "What do I need.?" I know she will not ask me again. She is better at playing the silent game than I am. She stops circling my heart and removes herself from me. She takes my hand and leads me to the two doors in the room. I open the door to the left; it is the bedroom door. The other door leads to the bathroom. I wait for her. She leads me to the bed and motions for me to lie down. She does not look at me. She takes in the contents of my room. There are clothes everywhere and empty bottles of liquor. She says nothing as she begins to clean. I can see her thinking.

This room is nothing like me. I am a neat freak. This is why I have a cleaning company that comes to my house every week. I like things in order, but by the look of this hotel suite, you would not know it. She picks up my clothes and puts them in a pile in the corner. She goes into the closet and sees that I have a couple of items hanging. She looks through the drawers and again finds a couple of items. She calls downstairs to the reservation desk. I can hear her one-sided conversation.

"Hello, I have a quick question. How long am I booked for?"

"Two more weeks?"

"Ok. Thank you."

She still does not look at me. She sits on the edge of the bed and begins to do something on her phone. When she has completed it, she picks up the room phone again and orders room service. Then, she finally allows her eyes to meet mine. Her eyes tell me the things she is not saying. She knows that I have not told her everything, and she is not going to ask. She knows that I want her here, but she will not take me lashing out at her. She knows me well, and she is very concerned. However, she will not push because she knows I don't want her to.

After this long non-verbal conversation, she says, "Room service will be here in 45 minutes. You will have clothes delivered in about 2 hours, and a laundry service is coming for those clothes." She points to the pile in the corner. "I need to call my office to make some arrangements since I will be gone for the rest of the week."

With that, she walks out of the room and closes the door. I run my hand down my face and sigh. *What do I do?*

Then I hear that soft confident voice of God say, "You could ask me?"

I shake my head. I think to myself, *"What if I am not ready for the answers?"*

God says, "Do you like how this is going?"

"No."

"Then, why not ask?"

"That house scares me."

"Because you know what is inside."

"Yeah…. her."

"And?"

"I don't know."

"Lying to me is not going to help."

"Fine, what I am looking for is in that house."

"So, just ask me."

I scratch my head and breathe deeply. This conversation is making me anxious. I don't get anxious often, but I do get anxious. Whatever is in that house is going to change my life. Maybe I just wait. But God is right; look where that has gotten me, alone, drinking, in my hometown, staying at a hotel, with shaky hands.

"Fine." I take a breath. *"Please show me. What are you trying to tell me?"*

"Peace, Beloved. I will show you when you are ready."

With that, I feel the peace of God wash over me. I have missed this feeling and His presence for quite a while. I have been drowning without Him. *"Thank you, God,"* I say, and with that, I fall asleep.

Chapter 4 – LeShay

"I know what it takes. Yes, I understand...... Do you think we can make it happen is the question......Ok. We will meet via Zoom next week. I should have some swatches and a tentative mood board or two by then...... Ok, sounds good...... Thank you." I take a breath.

My calls have gone from one to the office to two 30-minute troubleshooting calls. As I texted my assistant, letting her know that tomorrow morning I would need to speak with Dale, one of the other interior designers at my firm, there is a knock at the door. I go to open the door, and it is room service and the delivery guy with the clothes I ordered for Roe and me. I thank and tip the delivery guy as the room service server brings in our food. The server sets up the food on the bar counter, which I cleaned off during one of my calls, and I hang up the clothes in the hall closet. I tip the server as he leaves, and then I head to the bedroom to let Roe know that the food is here.

However, when I open the door, he is sleeping so peacefully. His curly mane is out of its usual slick ponytail, and it's sprawled across the bed. He looks so unruly that it makes me smile. I go and sit on the side of the bed and watch him sleep. This man means everything to me, and it is truly messing with my heart, my mind, and my spirit to know that he is emotionally and spiritually broken.

We have seen each other through some really difficult and messed-up situations, but this, this is something else. This is not physical or mental. I am almost one hundred percent sure this is all spiritual. Why Monroe refuses to deal with his spiritual issues until he has no choice, I don't know, but that has always been the case. Well, for at least as long as I have known him.

Years ago

"Why don't you just stop playing and admit that you don't know why you have that feeling, Roe?" I ask.

"Because that is admitting defeat. I am a doctor, Shay. I can figure this out."

"All things cannot be figured out with science. You know this."

"I am not in the mood for a spiritual conversation. My client is well, when she was dying just a few days ago. I can figure this out."

"OK, and when the labs still are just normal, and no treatment was added or taken away, you can come and tell me I was right. God did that." I say as I grab my bag and kiss the side of his head on my way out. Before I head out, he grabs me close and hugs me tight.

"Have a great day, and I will be calling once I figure it out to say you were wrong, Baby."

"Baby?"

"Yeah, Baby, Babe, Bae, Babes. Take a pick."

"So, that's what we are. Friends that call each other sweet endearments?"

His face goes serious, and he leans in and kisses that spot right in front of my ear and whispers, "Shay, you are my heart; that is true now, and my spirit says it will always be true. So, pick one or all of the above."

I smirk and reply, "OK. Any of them except Bae. Bae is for my man, which you are not."

"Understood, Babes." He starts laughing.

"By Baby, I got to go. You are making me late for class." I smile.

"See, you like the names." He kisses me again in the same place. Then, he returns to his laptop.

When he looks over his shoulder, I am at the door. I finally answer, "Yeah, you're right. It feels good. I like the names."

I smile at the memory of us and begin running my fingers through his curly mane. As I think about all the things he is to me, I pray silently, *God help me help him*. Then I hear God say, "You will." I continue to stroke his hair, and a feeling of peace runs through me. I lay my hand firmly but gently on top of his head and then place my other hand on his heart and allow God to use me.

I can feel God moving around us and between us. I can feel Monroe's spirit as he settles, and I feel it as peace takes a deeper root within him. As I am assessing when or if I should move, I feel Roe place his hands on mine. I allow some moments to pass, and then I open my eyes.

The dark brown eyes gazing into mine are the same confident, assured, and loving eyes that I saw on the day we met. He has found his peace again. I smile softly at him, and he pulls me to lie down with him.

After a little time, his deep sleep-laden voice comes through my fog of sleep, as I had started to drift off, "I miss this.... You and me." He speaks smoothly.

"I miss this too," I utter softly.

"I know you are falling asleep, but thank you for coming...... I needed...... Well, I needed you...." His voice trails off. This leads me to look up at him. When he looks down at me, instead of the confusion from before, there is resolve in his eyes. I sit up and move next to him. He sits up with his back against the headboard. He adjusts his shirt so that it is not bunched above his abs. He has on a dark green Bleu University T-shirt, which is our alma mater here in New Orleans. I wait for him to speak.

"I need to tell you the rest." He states calmly. His voice is throaty, raspy, and velvety all at once. It is smooth like honey but full bass. It causes me to slow down and move to his rhythm, no rushing just flowing. He knows the rest and this look in his eyes and the sound of his voice causes me to proceed just as slowly as the texture of his tone.

Eventually, I reply slowly with an "Ok" to his statement, while looking into his eyes.

He proceeds to tell me about what has been going on over the past year in his relationship with Kira and the dreams he has been having. Then he gets to the part where he tells me about the house and about sensing that I am inside the house. He pauses and tells me that he finally went inside of the house and saw an amazing chandelier and gallery in the master bedroom. The more he describes the house, the more I realize we had almost the exact same dream. The only difference is that he has been seeing everything that led up to my arrival at the house. He further tells me that the dream goes blank after seeing the paintings in the master bedroom. Then, the dream resumes with me in the kitchen making coffee and telling him about my itinerary for the day. He says he can hear kids coming down the stairs, but they don't make it to the kitchen. That is how his dream ends.

I take some deep breaths as he stares at me, waiting for my reaction to his disclosure. I don't know what to say. It's like the day we met all over again. We finally talked the night after we met. During that conversation, we learned that we both had the same dream, just different parts of the dream. He had laid the roses, and then the dream went blank. When the dream resumed, he was being pulled up by me, and roses were falling at his waist. Therefore, he did not see the roses like I did. This situation is the same. He saw the house and all the things happening before I got led to the house. His dream goes blank where mine picks up, and then where mine ends, his resumes. These are my thoughts as I am taking my deep breaths.

"You dreamt the same thing, didn't you?" He finally inquires through the silence. It is not an accusatory question; it is more of a realization.

I nod my head yes.

"Was there anything different?"

"You told me you needed me now. When I woke up, I called you. I did not dream about the kitchen or kids."

We stare into each other's eyes, waiting and observing the other.

"Rest with me, LeShay." With that, he pulls me into him, and we lay down again. Then I hear God say, "Stop stalling. Ask him what I said." I take some deep, calming breaths, again. I can feel they are not working, and my heart is beating faster. *God, I can't.* I pray silently. "You want to help? Ask him."

Monroe interrupts my conversation with God by saying, "Baby, just ask me." I shake my head no to his statement. He continues, "I can feel your heart beating and your anxious energy. Just ask."

"Why don't you just tell me?"

"Because I can't. We both have to want to know." He says calmly. He is rubbing his hand up and down my back in nice, relaxing strokes. He knows that relaxes my mind, body, and soul.

After a few moments, I finally ask the inevitable question, "What else happened in the dream, Monroe?"

"You kissed me and told me to have a great day, Bae."

"Bae?"

"Yep. When I looked down and took your hand, we both had wedding rings on our left ring finger. We kissed again, and then you left. I went to explore the rest of the house, and there were wedding photos of us. Photos of us when you were pregnant twice. Then, the children as they grew up. When I got to my study, there was a gorgeous painting of you hanging on the wall......"

I want to sit up and look at him, but I am scared. His voice is whimsical in a way I have never heard before. I stay silent. He continues, "There was a drafting table instead of a desk in the study. There were drawings of people and places. Then when I looked at the walls there were more paintings. There was canvas material and wood pieces in one corner and paint and other things in another corner. I realized there were no books in the study, which meant the room was my art studio more than a study. Then my phone rang, and it was you. I swiped to accept the call, and you said, 'Don't forget you have a meeting with the gallery today. Eric will be by to get you around 2p. Make sure you break something, Hot Stuff. See you tonight.' Then I woke up to your touch."

He takes a breath. He is calm, very calm. But me? I am freaking out. He is still stroking my back, and I am freaking out. He says, "Relax, Baby. Relax."

I finally sit up and look at him. "How are you calm right now? You just said..." I get up and start pacing. Shoot, is this what he has been thinking about? I may need a drink, a mix, or whatever he was taking yesterday.

"Baby..." He starts sitting up.

"No, no, no. Don't, Baby, me. You just said you dreamt that we were married with kids and you were a painter. A painter, and we live in our dream house with a purple door."

"I didn't say our dream house."

"Monroe, please! Everything about your dream and mine says the house we are talking about has everything you want and everything I want, including the overflowing love that comes when the couple is in sync."

He smirks. "Fair point."

"You think this is funny." I accuse him.

He gets up and walks toward me slowly. I back up because, no, this makes no sense. Eventually, my back hits the glass door that leads to the balcony. I fumble with the handle, and I cannot get it open so I can run further away from him or this or both. He finally reaches me, puts his hand over my head, and leans in.

"Breathe. LeShay Michelle Fontenot. Just Breathe, Baby." His voice comes off smooth, warm, and slow. It's like delicious chocolate melting in your mouth. Damn him. I relax almost instantly with him this close and his voice this deep...... Shoot...... I began to breathe slowly with him as he requested.

After some time, I finally speak a little more, well a lot more, calmer than before. I ask, "How are you this calm?"

"Truth?"

"Always," I answer with a smile.

He smiles back. He is still very much in my space, interesting. He says, "Truth is, I have always known it was you. You would be the one I spent my life with. I just didn't know that meant we would be married with kids. But for some reason, that too makes sense."

He has moved closer in, but we are not touching. I'm at a loss, really. Then he says, "Say something. Please."

"Why are you so close?" I ask. He looks down where we are almost touching, and it is like he just realized how close we are standing. I push at his chest gently, and he moves back a little. Truth is we sit and stand close all the time, but right now, it feels like the energy, the space, the chemistry, whatever you want to call it, is different, which makes our proximity mean more than just standing closely.

His gaze returns to mine. "Monroe Marquis Thibodeaux, why are you looking at me like that?" He has never looked at me the way he is looking at me now. He is observing me, but it is more than that. It is like an appraisal. He is perusing my face instead of just looking at it. He is examining me thoroughly with his eyes. His breathing has changed.

Look, I am not stupid by any means. I get it. My best friend is currently checking me out, but this has never been a thing before. It is the reason we can be so close, and it not be a thing. He is a very gorgeous man, but that is not us. I gently push him back and sidestep him. "Monroe?"

"We kissed in my dream, and it was the most amazing feeling I have ever had. It was like I was home mixed with the most erotic pleasure I have ever felt."

"It was a dream. It was supposed to be all of that."

He gazes deep into my eyes. Oh no, I turn around and head into the living space. "So, what do you plan to do with all these paintings?"

He starts laughing, like crying laughing. "Wow, you not gone even try and be subtle?"

"What for, you aren't?"

"Naw…" He gets serious again, and then he starts tracking me with his eyes. I move around organizing things I have already organized. I feel like the prey, and my predator is coming. Sure enough, he stalks toward me and corners me against the wall. "Shay, have you ever dreamt about us the way I said?"

"Like what?" I try for coy and look away.

He raises my chin so my eyes have to meet his. Then he asks again, very smooth, sensual, and dark. It is a tone I have never heard from him before. One that makes me want to crawl into his skin. *What the entire hell?* I think to myself. I cannot help but look into his eyes because he is still holding my chin in place. I finally breathe, and he grins.

"Fine, yes.... But we did more than kiss."

"More?" He asks inquisitively with a smirk.

"Yes."

"How much more?"

"Everything."

"Everything covers a lot of ground, Shay."

"There was a reason I would not visit you last Christmas or New Year's."

"That's why you were dodging my calls." His voice is getting huskier by the minute. I cannot do this with him. He must sense my inclination to run rising because he cages me in with both his arms on either side of my head.

"Monroe, please..."

"Please, what?

"Stop..."

"I haven't done anything......"

"You know what I am saying."

"Why didn't you tell me?"

"Because you had a girlfriend, and we don't do this." I point between us. "I figured I was just trippin'."

"You knew you were not trippin'."

"Baby, please."

"Please, what?"

"We can't do this. We…. can't do this."

"What is this?"

"Baby…"

"Tell me…" He leans in closer so that his body is pressed against mine. I can feel him, all of him. His member included, and I promise I almost shiver from the pleasure of his closeness. He is such a predator at this moment because as he takes in the sight of me flustered and bothered, his grin spreads slowly and intoxicating-ly across his face. He knows what he is doing to me.

"We can't kiss or have sex or any of that. You are my best friend. My confidant. My peace. My protector. You can't be all that and my lover. My life does not work that way." I push at his chest, but this time, he does not move back. Instead, he pushes me further into the wall and bends to whisper in my ear.

"But what if I could be…." He then steps back slightly, and I take a grounding breath. "What if we could be all the things that happened in my dream, in our dream? What if that is exactly what we are supposed to be? Friends, Lovers, Married."

"Do you even want to get married? Every time one of your girlfriends brings it up, it is like you are going to die. Kira was the first one you didn't shut down, immediately."

"Fair point, but I never said I did not want to get married. I said I did not know how that would fit with my life vision."

"Ok, well, I don't recall your life vision changing."

"True, but what if it is supposed to?"

"You want to risk us on what-ifs, Roe?"

"No, I want to risk us on what we both know is a God-given sign."

"Ok, fine. It is, but what if it is metaphorical and not literal?"

"Oh, ok. So, now, you want to play me. Don't do me, LeShay. You know as well I do that this dream is not metaphorical. In fact, let's just be honest for once. This whole time has not been metaphorical. We are both just too afraid to take a risk with this." He points between the two of us and begins pacing.

"No, we have both been busy. We both have goals and life visions that we want to accomplish. We just don't make time for relationships that mean anything to us in the romance department." I bite back.

"Oh, that's what you're telling yourself these days?"

"Don't say it like I am lying to myself. I'm not. Do you not have goals that have caused you to put any and all meaningful romantic relationships to the side?"

"Yes, of course I do…"

I interrupt him. "See. So, how would this even work out? You sabotage good relationships."

"Wow, so you are trying to do me. Got it. Look..." I had pressed a nerve accidentally but pressed it all the same. At this point, he had stopped pacing and was stalking back toward me. This time, cornering me against the counter. "Hear me clear, LeShay. I have never sabotaged a relationship. I have intentionally dated people I saw no future with until Kira. But this," He points between him and me. "This right here has never been sabotaged. In fact, I have left very important meetings, rounds, and network opportunities to come to you, LeShay. You are the only one who I have ever cared enough for to stop what I am doing because you need me. And you do the same for me. No," As I shake my head, he puts a finger against my lips, "Enough. The proof is in the fact that you are here right now. You forget I know where you are supposed to be today and for the rest of the week. You are supposed to be in LA closing one of the biggest deals of your career. But where are you right now? Here with me. Why? Because I needed you. So, don't do me. I would move through hell and high water for you, which also means the only person I would marry if I did marry is you. There, I said it." With that, he backs up, lifts his eyebrow, and looks at me like checkmate.

Right now, we are having a stare-off, and we are both breathing hard. This man.... I don't have any words.

Minutes pass before he asks, "Cat got your tongue, LeShay?" Then, he smirks and moves back into my space, pressing his body flush against mine with my butt pressed into the counter. He gently picks up my size 10 frame and places me on the counter. I watch him as he opens my red jogger-clad legs and moves to stand comfortably between them. He places one hand on either side of me and then presses his forehead to mine. I can smell the hint of his custom body wash. It is a mix of apple and cedarwood. It is rich and enticing, with slight hints of sweetness underneath. It is the perfect reflection of who he is. He is all confident, strong, and loyal, and then kind, affectionate, and loving. I have never understood why these women who date him have a problem.

Then I think about what he just said and how the characteristics that he gives me, he doesn't actually give to anyone else. He will hold my hand and hug me close in public and private without a thought, and I receive and return that affection every time, just like now. With his girlfriends in the past, he did not do PDA, and then his job always came first. But like he said, with me, that is not the case.

We are intertwined in a very intimate space; he rubs his nose across mine and then hugs me close. We have never been in this position, so for the first time, I can feel the full strength of him, that strength that comes when your man lifts you and holds you close before taking you hard. Anyway, I gaze up into his eyes as he begins to put space between us. I know he wants me to speak. I just don't know. This is all new.

"Shay, I know I could make you talk to me right now, but that is not what I want. I need you to tell me your thoughts on your own accord. That being said, I will wait until you are ready to discuss this. Openly." He states it with finality. Then, he turns around. I know him well enough to know that as generous as that statement sounded, it was not. He is making a boundary with me and putting distance between us. I can feel him walling off his heart the further he walks away from me. I can't have that. He is…. I don't have the words to describe the depth of importance he has to me.

"Wait," I say as I get off the counter. He turns to look at me, guard to his heart setting in place. "Please don't do this."

"What?" He asks calmly.

"You know what. You are walling yourself off from me. We don't do that."

"LeShay, I can't; we cannot act like I didn't say what I just said. I know you are processing, and I will not stop that. But I can't and won't take back what I said. What I said needs and deserves a response."

"I know," I say meekly and drop my head.

He walks back to me and lifts my chin, "Baby, I will always be here. I just…"

I can see the confusion and feelings of abandonment coursing across his soul. His childhood wasn't bad, but he did have issues. Shoot, we all do on some level. His issue is abandonment, and my not responding is triggering him. And, I am not good with that.

Taking a breath, I smile slightly and decide to be transparent. "Monroe…. I'm scared. I'm scared of what it would be like to be with you, to be your woman. I fear what will happen to us if you and I cross that line from friends to lovers. I am scared that if we do this, if I fully give myself to you, I will lose myself, because I know loving you will be better than anything I have ever experienced. I am scared, Baby…" I turn away from him. I hate feeling so vulnerable, and he knows this.

He turns me around to face him once more and lifts my chin. As he gazes into my eyes, he says, "You don't have to be scared with me. We would be in the same place. And let's be clear, I will not let you lose yourself in me, just like you won't let me lose myself in you."

"What do you want from me?"

"One kiss. Then, we see what happens."

"You just got out of a relationship."

"Stop stalling. Are we kissing or what?"

"That invitation. Sucks." We both laugh. "One kiss?"

"One."

Sighing audibly, I nod my head in agreement. This one kiss is about to change everything, and I can feel that. But, I also know he is right. We can not pretend that he did not say what he said, because that in itself changed some things.

Chapter 5 – Monroe

I know she is not ready for more than a kiss. Shoot, I am not sure if I am ready for more. I know my future will be with her, however. My dream was clear and vivid. God said everything I needed to hear. LeShay is my treasure, my sweet thang from on high, and it is my choice to do something or not. To be honest, LeShay has had me since the first time we met at Da Spot. Her mind, body, and soul have captivated and inspired me on many occasions. This kiss is about to change things, but if I am right, which I am, it will change for the better.

I walk into her space and lift her chin. Her eyes tell me to be gentle and that she is nervous, but she trusts me. I lean in the 90% and hover, waiting for her to take the final leap. She leans in, and we kiss. At first, the kiss is soft. The feeling of her lusciously plump, velvety lips makes me lean in further. When I tilt my head to the side, she does the same and opens her mouth slightly. Taking the offer, I mimic her motion and suck her bottom lip between mine lips. She tastes like strawberries and sweet crème. It's intoxicating and addictive. I want more.

I slide my tongue into her mouth, and she meets my tongue with hers. We slide our tongues across each other, feeling and exploring one another in a way that was forbidden before. I pull her into me, and she molds into me the way she always does, but now it feels inebriating. I want to fuse myself with her and become this intricate, intimate design of just us. I have never wanted to inhale someone before, but boy, do I want to right now. She wraps her arms around my neck and plays with the hair at the nape of my neck. She pulls me closer as if she wants the same thing I do, as if she wants to consume and mesh with my being.

When she moans into my mouth, I cannot hold it anymore. I pick her up in one swoop, and she wraps her marvelous legs and thighs around me. I push her into the wall and devour her mouth. She matches me, lip for lip, tongue for tongue. I moan into her, and she moans into me. My hands are palming her deliciously, round and ample ass. My hips begin to grind into her of their own accord. I cannot hide that my dick is ram-rod hard and so ready. I feel the heat coming off of her center. I should stop, but it's like I can't. I have found my favorite place, dessert, meal, and life source, and I don't want to leave.

We keep doing this dance until the need for oxygen overtakes us. I pull my mouth away from hers and rest my forehead against hers. We breathe in each other's air. Eventually, our breathing slows, and we breathe in sync. She wraps her legs tighter around me and pulls my head closer. I pull her into me and hug her tightly, enjoying the feel of her body against mine, allowing the sensation of this moment to take root in my mind, body, and soul. I am 100% sure that LeShay is my woman. If I had any doubts before, there are none now. My entire being is humming mine as I hold her, and I agree she is mine.

Her eyes are closed as we breathe together. I feel her heartbeat as she allows it to slow and meet mine. She is not sleeping, but she is hiding from me. I walk us to the sofa and sit with her, straddling my lap. When she tries to move off, I steady her in place. I use one hand and rub it gently on her cheek. Allowing her shoulder-length locs to fall over my fingertips. When she leans to the side and rests her cheek in my palm, I stroke her cheek with my thumb and then say, "Shay, Baby......" My voice is vulnerable even to my ears.

She opens her caramel-colored eyes immediately. The sight I see in their depths takes my breath away and makes my heart skip a beat. She's in love with me. She's in love with me. There is no mistaking it. No, questioning it. How did I miss this? When did this happen? She keeps gazing into my eyes, allowing me to see the truth of her love and loyalty to me. I realize at this moment that there is usually a wall in her gaze that stops me from seeing this part of her. I can't help myself; I use my hands to pull her face into mine and kiss her gently, lovingly, and completely, trying to tell her everything I have yet to say.

When we pull away, she takes a deep breath. Then she says, "I love you, Babes." She smirks. I smirked in return but said nothing so she could finish. She continues, "I have loved you since the first picnic we shared on the yard. I fell in love with your laugh and your spirit, with you." She shakes her head and tries to get up. I hold her firmly in place because I will not let her run from this.

She holds my gaze, trying to test my resolve. I win, so she continues. Shaking her head, she says, "But even with that, I can't do this with you. Not now.".

"Why not?" I ask slowly as anguish begins to rise within me.

"Because there is still so much I want to do before I settle down with someone."

"So, your career?"

"Yes, that will be your answer too."

"No, it won't."

"Baby, your career is always first, and you haven't accomplished your life vision yet, so..."

"LeShay, I want you. Period. Whatever that means and entails."

"Monroe..."

"Tell me the real why, not the excuse you give everyone else. The real reason. The one you would only give me."

She takes a long pause. "I'm scared of love. I'm scared to truly give myself to someone, especially the way that I would give myself to you. Monroe, I can't risk messing us up and no longer having you in my life."

"So, you would rather not try for something amazing and just settle for something mediocre."

"That's not fair. Our friendship is great. It is not mediocre."

"Compared to what just happened between us. Yes, it is. What just happened says there is so much more we have not even begun to touch. LeShay..."

"I can't, Monroe. I can't." She starts crying and shaking her head. She gets up and picks up her purse to leave. I rush to the door before she can open it.

"Where are you going?"

"I need a moment." She turns and faces me. "Monroe, I love you. I do. But I can't do this with you. I can't."

"Why not with me? LeShay..."

"No." She states firmly and opens the door. I allow it and watch her walk down the hall to the elevator.

I know that this moment has just changed everything. For the first time, we are not on the same page, and there is no compromise to be made. *God help.* I pray silently.

Part 2: I Choose You:

Five Years Later

Chapter 6 – LeShay

"Gurl, you sure you want to do this?" Sena asks me as I move around my bedroom, packing my clothes.

"I know you *really* like Antoine, but moving in together is a big deal," Carmen states.

"I more than *really* like Antoine. I love him, and I want to be with him. This is the next step for us."

"What happened to 'I want to be married one day and never want to do the cohabitation thing'?" Sena questions me again while mimicking my prior statement. I stop packing and turn to look at my gurls. They are concerned. I get it. A lot has changed in the last year and a half.

So I take a breath, sit on my bare mattress, and make eye contact with them both, so they know I am serious. "Ladies, I love y'all. I do, and I get that you are worried. But I am good. Selling my portion of my interior design firm was a good move for me, just like moving in with Antoine is, too. I am happy. Can y'all please be happy for me?" I smile sweetly as I ask the question.

They look at each other and shake their heads, then roll their eyes and smile my way. Sena says, "You know we got you, and we will be happy for you if this is truly what you want."

"It is, and I'm good. Promise." I reassure them.

"Ok, so when do the movers get here?" Carmen asks.

"In 3 hours, so we better finish."

We share a quick hug and then get back to work.

****

After everything in my room was packed, we headed downstairs to my kitchen, which was full of boxes. Most of the boxes will be moved to storage, as Antoine does not have enough space for both of our belongings. When I decided to move in with him, I knew that I would have to find something to do with my stuff, so storage is what it is.

Not only am I moving in with Antoine, but I am also selling my house. I think it is the fact that I chose to sell my house and sell my portion of the firm that truly has my friends spooked. See my gurls, they don't like Antoine. They think he is too conservative and not flexible enough in his mentality. I know he can be a little rigid, but that helps balance me out. I tend to get a little too unorthodox sometimes, too out of the box, some would say.

My gurls questioned me multiple times about moving in with him, but they did not become truly adamant about me taking my time and thinking it through until I told them I was also selling my house. They said I should keep the house as it gave me somewhere to return to if things did not go well with Antoine.

As I look around my house, the truth is, I do not want to return to this house. Just like I did not want to return to the interior design firm once I stopped enjoying it and lost my passion for the art and process of design. What I have not told Sena and Carmen is that one day I woke up and realized I had no pleasure in coming home to my house that I paid good money for, and I realized I did not find any joy in the company that I had worked so hard to co-create. Honestly, it was on that day that I became fully aware that things in my life needed to change.

However, the other truth is that I don't know what the change needs to be. By moving in with Antoine, I buy myself time to figure it all out and be with the man I love, simultaneously. Antoine and I are growing together, and I like that. Figuring out what is next is not just about steps but also about vision. I need vision for what is next and time to plan out the steps. This all takes time, prayer, thinking, and research, which is why I decided not to go straight into looking for another job but to take the moment and really think about what I want and need right now.

So, here I am, moving out of my home and moving into my boyfriend's house. I collected a nice check from selling my portion of the firm, and I put some into savings and invested some. Now, as I figure things out, I have a nest egg as well as time. I love that my boyfriend is on board with this plan. If he has his way, I will not return to work at all, and we will get married soon. He would have me just give him babies and stay at home, but I don't know about all of that.

As I am thinking about these things, I feel my phone vibrate with a text message. It is the movers. I guess this is it. I am about to move into my next, whatever that is.

Chapter 7 – LeShay

"Dale, I understand that, but you do realize I am no longer your boss or your colleague. You need to tell Shawn this. She will help you; I promise... I know. I won't hold it against you. Plus, you got this.... Ok, bye." I say, ending the call. "I'm sorry, Antoine. I know, no work calls during dinner." I gaze into his eyes and smile.

"You've been gone from your firm for almost 6 months. I thought they would have figured out how to operate without you by now." He speaks with a chill lacing his voice. He hates work calls during dinner. He thinks that once he gets home, everything should be all about him. I get it, but things don't always work out that way.

I try to smooth things over. I lean in toward him and softly say, "Sweetheart, I know. Soon, ok? They are finishing the last of the projects that I spearheaded. My exit contract says I have to stay available until they finish that.... But enough talk about that. How was your day?"

He relaxes now that all of my attention is focused on him. Then, He begins, "Pretty good. I was thinking maybe we should redecorate my house so it looks like our house. What do you think?"

Truly, it sounds like work to me, but he is excited, so I go with it. "Umm, ok." I smile.

"Great." He returns to eating his food, and we finish eating the rest of dinner in silence.

I have been living with Antoine for about three months now. It's weird that, as much as we have hung out and spent time together before cohabitating, I did not realize how little he actually talks. It is like when we are on dates or hanging out outside of home, he talks a lot. But when we get home, he has nothing to say or only has one or two-word sentences. I did bring this up to him during our first few weeks of living together, but he told me it was probably because he had not lived with someone in ten years. I get that, but I feel like something should have changed at least a little since it has been three months.

Anyway, when we are done eating dinner, I take the dishes and put them in the dishwasher, and he goes to take a shower. As I am rinsing out the pots, I think about the life I am living now. It is entirely different from the life I thought I would be living and the life I was living a year ago. On the one hand, I honestly believed that I would love the hustle and bustle of owning my own business and climbing the ranks to become a millionaire, but it was not all it was cracked up to be. I realize now that I like the slower pace of things, being intentional, and in the moment with everything I do—the way I used to be before the firm. However, even with my re-found intentionality, I am missing something, and I cannot quite figure out what it is.

These are my thoughts as I am finishing the dishes. Once I am done, I head to the living room with a glass of wine. As I sit on the sofa with my glass of white wine and watch my favorite reality couples show, I can hear Antoine coming back down. He grabs his pre-poured, by moi, glass of Jake and Coke off the counter and heads my way. He sits next to me so that our thighs are touching, and he places his arm around me. I finish my wine and set the glass on the wooden coffee table. I lean my head on his chest as he hugs me closer, and we watch the show. We do this *every* night. Seriously, *every* night. The truth is, this should be relaxing, right? But....again, something is not quite complete or satisfying.

The next morning is more of the same routine. Every day is the same thing, but not in that routine brings me comfort and stability, kind of way. I cannot shake this feeling. There is this unseen half-empty glass that is sitting inside of me, when I should be full and relaxed.

Anyway, every morning, I make him avocado toast with no salt or pepper and a cup of black coffee. He sits at the bar and reads the New York Times on his phone. I drink my double-shot caramel macchiato with oat milk and extra foam from my espresso machine, and I watch him.

This morning, as I observe him reading, the feeling of neutrality annoys me. Is this the life I want? I know I don't want life to be fast and stressful, but do I really want things to be this slow and unremarkable? So mundane and monotonous?

As I reach the halfway point in my macchiato, he looks up, winks at me, and then goes back to reading just like he does every morning. Then it hits me clear as day, no, this is not it, either. What am I doing? Maybe I just need a job. My life cannot be all about him and this house; perhaps that is my issue. Maybe it is not him but me.

With this in mind, I clear his empty dishes and put them in the dishwasher. Then, like every other morning, I meet him at the door and kiss him goodbye. Again, yet more of the same things every day. Maybe I do need to find a job or just get out of the house. As I watch him drive off, I decide that today will be different. I will be going out. After all, redecorating this house and looking for furniture may help.

After shutting the door, I go upstairs, put on a lightweight, possibly see-through in the sun, deep purple maxi dress, and let my waist-length locs hang freely. After spraying some refresher in my hair, I put on a little concealer, blush, purple shimmery eyeshadow, and a nude lip gloss. Next, I spray on my custom sweet musk perfume that mixes perfectly with my body chemistry, allowing me to smell and feel sensual and alluring. Lastly, I put on my sparkly nude sandals and matching purse. Looking myself over, I pick up one of my crystal-encrusted hair sticks and twist my locs into a messy bun. I finish my outfit by placing a long silver and rose gold necklace on my neck, which hangs in the middle of my cleavage, and inserting the matching large hoops into my pierced ears. Now, I am ready to go.

Stopping by the downstairs mirror, I take one last glance and notice that I'm looking like a baddie, if I don't say so myself. Today, I am very much tapping into a vibe I have not been in for some time. Too long a time, if I am being honest. I look myself in the eye and smile. After a moment, I give myself a wink and head out to my Tanzanite Blue BMW X4 M40i with custom silver/black 20" rims. As I get into my SUV, I think about what my gurls said before I moved in with Antoine.

I have begun to question if they are right. Is Antoine too conservative for me? I don't think so, and I am not one to blame my issues on someone else. I am not ready to agree with them yet, because I have not exhausted the me factor. Right now, I really think I need something to do instead of hanging around the house all day. Maybe staying home is just not my thing. I mean, I am the person who was previously involved in any and everything, professionally and personally. I have never been the one to just sit at home. So, why did I think I could do that now?

As I think about these things, I back out of the driveway and head nowhere in particular. I allow my thoughts to continue flowing and processing as I drive along. Before I realize it, I am parking my car in front of my old Yoni Steam Spa, Miraculous Bliss. Interesting. I look around at the changes to the business park/Strip Mall where the Yoni Spa sits. Now, there is the Spa, then a chakra reading place next door, and then a crystal spot. Umm, interesting.

This is the side of town where I bought my townhouse when I got my first *real* job. I was so excited to work at Houston's largest and most prominent interior design firm. It was a starting position, and I had to work hard. But I was happy to do the grind. After all, I had goals. I had my life vision. Now, some twelve years later, here I am, back where I started. Well, more like starting over.

Yeah, a Yoni Steam may be just what I need to figure out what is happening with me. Yoni steaming tends to make me feel grounded and reflective. It provides a safe space to connect with what is happening internally. *Thank you, God. You always know what I need.* I pray silently.

I get out of my SUV and head into the Spa. When I open the door, the smell of roses and sandalwood fills my nostrils. It makes me feel calm and sensual. It actually goes with my vibe today. When I get to the reception desk, I ask if they have any openings for a walk-in. She told me I was in luck because their 9 am was just canceled. So, I was right on time.

Sitting on the yoni steam seat in the crème and deep blue yoni room with pictures of silhouettes of beautiful black women, I sip my lavender and mint-infused water. I begin to think about the last five years. It has been a crazy rollercoaster. I left Monroe standing outside the W Hotel the day after we kissed. There was no way for us to return to what we were before everything he said, and he was right.

I think about how everything just started to feel uncomfortable and how my dreams even got weird after I left him in New Orleans. It was like, after that, God began pointing out everything in my life that was out of place, from my job to my house to the side of town I lived on to the co-workers and associates I spoke with every day, and now to my boyfriend, if I am being honest.

When I met Antoine three years ago, it was refreshing because he knew what he wanted, and he was stable. He was not trying to change anything. He was right where he was supposed to be. I liked the continuity and the consistency. I liked that I did not have to guess with him or wonder what would happen next. After all, he was always where the calendar app said he would be, and he always said the same things.

Now, though, I think I liked all of those things about him because I was running from all the changes happening around and within me. However, now that I am not running, I am becoming more stable internally. Well, that might not be true. I need to figure this out, figure me out, and figure out what I am supposed to do now and quickly, because this current internal space I am in is becoming increasingly irritating.

"You could just ask me." I hear God say.

"You could just tell me," I respond internally with slight sass and sarcasm.

"I did," God replies, ignoring my attitude.

"No, you didn't."

"So, I am lying?"

"God, that is not what I said." Shoot, that is basically what I said. *"Ok, sorry. No, I don't think you are lying. I just don't remember knowing what my next move is supposed to be?"*

"Roe?"

"God, I don't mean that."

"I do."

I let out a long sigh. Really, what does He want me to do with that? I have not spoken to Roe in five years. I don't even know if his number is the same.

Then, I hear God say, "It is."

"So, what...... I should call and say what? I quit my job, sold my house, and now, I don't know what to do with myself."

"And..."

"And I'm living with my boyfriend, which is something I said I would never do, and I low-key am not enjoying it."

"And…"

"And, what?"

"I miss you."

"What good would that do?"

"Start there, Beloved."

With that, the yoni steam practitioner comes in and tells me that my time is up. I get up and dry off using the plush, deep ocean blue towel. As I do, I think about my conversation with God just now. I could say what God told me to say, but it has been so long….I don't know.

I put back on my dress, use some travel-size perfume to reactivate my signature scent, and head to the checkout desk. After I am done at Miraculous Bliss, I decide to take a walk to the crystal shop at the end of this part of the strip. The way my life is hitting me at the moment, a new crystal may be just what I need.

When I walked into the shop, I realized it was not a crystal shop at all, but a furniture store called Love It, Own It. The shop is a whole vibe. It feels like you walked into destiny, laced with let's get to work energy. It is warm and inviting, but at the same time invigorating and choice-provoking. As I look around, I see an array of different kinds of custom-built luxury furniture pieces, but not regular furniture, like for your house. It is the kind of furniture that would go well in a spiritual healing center or spa. There are beautifully designed chaises, end tables, chairs, fixtures, and everything you could need in various sizes and shapes. No two pieces are the same. Each piece has its own unique existence and purpose. I am genuinely loving this place.

As I am gliding my hand across one of the purple velvet chaises, admiring how soft yet firm it is, one of the shop employees walks up to me. She says, "Hello, I thought I would give you a minute. My name is Mari, and I am one of the Floor Specialists here. Can I help you find something?"

"No, I am just looking. But quick question. Who is this store geared towards?" I ask as I feel my internal interior designer rising and meshing with my intuitive side. Interesting, this feeling has never happened before.

"Well, anyone can make a purchase, of course, but we specialize in furniture for spiritual healing businesses like the ones in this business park," Mari replies gently yet confidently.

"I see...And all of the pieces are customized, right?"

"Yes, you have a good eye."

I smile and say, "Thanks. I am an interior designer. Well, I was an interior designer. Long story. Anyway, do you happen to have any Reiki tables?"

"Yes, of course. Right this way." She states excitedly as she turns to lead the way.

I followed her to the back of the store, touching different pieces along the way. I am not sure why I asked about Reiki tables, as I don't need one; however, I will go with this train of thought for now.

As we walked through the store, I noticed multiple sections throughout the open concept layout. I glance across the sections, trying to take in the things we pass that sit in the distance or out of reach. Mari was right. This store has everything you need to open a spiritual healing spa or studio. There are even huge genomes of different gemstones.

After she showed me where the Reiki tables are, she left me, providing me some privacy to browse through the Reiki furniture options. Before I get more into exploring the Reiki tables, I decide to take a detour to the giant genomes we passed. Something about them makes me need a second look.

When I get to the section with multiple genomes, I realize there is a room off to the side. I feel the draw, the pull of energy. But what makes me move is when my spirit jumps, letting me know I need to go there. So, I walk over to the room. When I peek inside, I find different genomes housed in one small space. I step fully inside the room, and once I do, it feels like I am snugly wrapped in a hug of pure energy emanating from the different stones. The energetic hug feels stabilizing and grounding. I find myself taking a seat on the floor and taking a meditative pose without thinking about it. It is like my spirit reflexed into the posture it knows for relaxation and seeking God. I close my eyes and take some deep breaths. *God help me.* I pray. I can feel God's presence before I hear Him say, "I told you to speak to Roe." I take some more deep breaths. I think about what God is saying. *Fine, I will.* I pray.

As I inhale and exhale deeply once more and allow the calm of God's presence to ease my tension, I decide, ok, I can call Roe. I mean, we are still friends. I take a moment and let myself be wrapped in peace, and allow myself to garner more strength to call my best friend after all this time.

As I reach my space of resolve in the fact that I will call Roe, I prepare to get up. However, before I can open my eyes, the energy in the room shifts. It's like home and sex just walked into the room. I inhale deeply, and the scent of apple and cedarwood fills my senses. Oh, my God! It can't be...... But I know it is.

Chapter 8 – Monroe

I was on my way to work when I heard God tell me to take a detour. He kept telling me where to turn until I ended up in front of a shop called Love It, Own It. Why He brought me here, I had no clue, but I followed instructions and went inside. As soon as I stepped into the shop, I knew why I was there. It wasn't the furniture. She was there, somewhere. I could feel the sweetness of home that only she brought to my spirit, but I also sensed desperation and confusion.

As I assessed this truth, the Floor Specialist introduced herself. "Hi, I am Mari. Can I assist you with finding furniture today?"

"Actually, I am looking for someone. A woman with locs." That is, if she still has locs, I think the latter to myself. It has been five years. For all I know, she cut them off. I hear God say, "She didn't cut them." Well, at least that is still true.

Mari's face lights up, "Yes, she is back this way. I can take you."

"No, I can find her. Please, just point me in the right direction." She points toward the back and to the right.

The further back I walk, the more intense I can feel her energy. I should not be surprised that God would lead me to her today. I have been dreaming about her a lot lately. At first, I was mad that God wanted to talk about her. After all, she did walk out on me, and we have not spoken since. I tried to call and text back then, but eventually, I stopped. We could not return to what we were. I had ruined that, which is something that I have had to live with.

Anyway, I kept walking until I saw a room filled with crystal genomes. I can't help but walk that way as I feel this pull of energy and a jump in a spirit that all says go there. When I reach the open door and look inside, I see her sitting on the floor in meditation. The dent in her forehead says that whatever God is saying, she is not interested in hearing. But then the dent vanishes, she rolls her shoulders back, and she relaxes. It is then that my spirit feels led to enter the space fully. As soon as I enter the room, I am consumed with the grounding energy of the crystals, but also the relaxation of home and the sensual energy of pure, unadulterated sex. I take a few breaths. This latter feeling is new. What happened to the confusion? I can still feel her desperation, but it is not as high. It is almost like she finally agreed to do whatever God was asking. Interesting.

I see her take a breath. I can tell the moment she realizes that it is I who just walked into the room. There is an expression of shock, then hesitation. I take a step that positions me to stand directly before her. Then, I wait for her to open her eyes; as I wait, I take out my phone and text my team, letting them know I will be late today.

As I pocket my phone, she opens her eyes, and my heart melts. Her eyes are filled with regret and longing and a little hope. I find myself instinctively taking a seat on the floor with her and taking her hands in mine. We stare into each other's eyes and examine each other's bodies and faces, looking to see what has changed. When my eyes return to her caramel-colored ones, I say, "Hey, Baby."

It is like that is all she needed me to do in order for her to do what she does next. She gets up and climbs into my lap, wrapping her legs and arms around me. She holds me close. I slowly stroke her back in that way that makes her relax and lean closer into me. I inhale her scent. She has on a new perfume. It is sensual and deep with a slight sweetness. It almost makes her smell... edible. I love it. Interesting.

With her wrapped around me, we stay this way for a moment, allowing our present selves to get to know each other spiritually. There is always a spiritual interchange that happens between us when we see one another. It is like our spirits need to share a hug, to feel the full presence of the other. I won't lie; it also feels good to have her physically in my arms as well.

She leans back with her hands still around my neck, and she smiles. The kind of smile that reaches her eyes and transforms her face. The smile that lets me know she is glad that I am here with her. We gaze into each other's eyes for a long time, allowing the other to see past the surface. I want to protect myself from what I know she will see. The truth is, I love this woman. My dreams have not changed over the past five years. They have only become more intense and more detailed. I have seen portions of our future lives together, along with things that I needed to change within me in order to be ready for life with her.

When she left me in New Orleans, I was pissed. I mean, how could she? She knew my issues with abandonment. Too many people that I have loved have walked out on me, starting with my father, then my grandmother, then my first love. So yeah, abandonment issues are one of the things that I have had to work on regularly over the past five years.

When she left New Orleans, I had to really dig deep and understand that she wasn't abandoning me but protecting herself and us in her own way. Eventually, I calmed down enough for God to show me that I wasn't ready for the life He had revealed to me in my dream, that neither one of us was. He began to show me what I needed to change about my priorities and my life vision to become ready for the life He had revealed to me. His vision. He showed me how my life vision was just that, my vision, and that I had never really asked Him for His vision for my life, my overall purpose in life. When I finally worked up the courage to ask, He showed me things I had never even dreamt of, things that put me in awe and exhilarated me. I won't lie; changing my life vision to follow what God said was tough, but it has definitely been worth it.

After all, now, I am sitting with my treasure in my lap and staring into her eyes. Eyes, I have not seen in way too long. I stroke a stray loc behind her ear and notice the blonde and purple highlights that were not there before. She dips her head, hiding the blush I know has risen. This is why I did it: because I know how much the action affects her.

She looks back up at me and says, "Hey, Baby."

Her voice is low and warm, like a caress to my heart. I smirk and reply. "Hey."

"Fancy seeing you here."

"Is it?" I respond with a smirk.

She stares at me for a moment and shakes her head to stop her own smirk from forming. Then, she says more solemnly, "I'm sorry about New Orleans and everything after. I should have answered your texts... I just didn't know how to move forward. I know you needed me to respond; I just couldn't find the words to say what I needed to say..."

I stop her mid-sentence by saying, "Baby, I know. I am not mad. Well, not anymore. We were not ready. It was not the time to move on what I saw; that was on me. We were just supposed to be aware. I'm sorry, too."

"You don't need to apologize."

"Yes, I do. I pushed us to make a move when we should have waited."

"True." She says as she smiles softly.

"How about we figure out how friendship will look now?" I suggest with a slight smile.

"You still want to be friends?"

"You don't?"

"Well, I do, but your dream. Has it changed?"

"No."

"So...how can you just be friends with me?"

"Because it is not time, and I can be patient. I need you in my life, even as just my friend. Because this living without you situation... sucks."

"Yeah, it does." We laugh. Then, she adds, "Ok. So, friends?"

We shake hands, as I reply, "Friends."

Then she surprises me and says, "When it is time to discuss the rest, we will. Ok?"

"The rest?" I question while lifting an eyebrow.

"I may or may not agree with you about the potential future. When I am clear on my end, we can talk. Ok?"

Well, this is new. She is not clear about the future of us, but she is not opposed to there being an us. Interesting. What is going on with her? I post the question internally to myself. I wonder if that is why I am here. Everything in my spirit is like Bingo.

So, I say, "Ok……now, would you like to discuss why you are meditating in the middle of a furniture store?"

Chapter 9 – LeShay

Oh, how I missed Roe. He looks absolutely fantastic, and his new facial hair is extremely attractive. He has always been freshly shaven, the no mustache or beard type, but now he has a low-cut beard that frames his masculine jaw line in a smooth layer of healthy short hair. His curly mane appears longer and is pulled back out of his face with a hair tie. He looks good, and that calm, grounding peace that is his presence is in full swing. This is precisely what I needed today: some peace.

"Shay?" He asks.

"Sorry, I was thinking."

"About?" He questions.

Really, I was examining his face, but that is not the point right now. We are friends. But damn, if I do not find him tantalizing in a way I never have before. I am not going to say that, though; so instead, the words I speak are, "Long story. I'm sure you don't have time." I smile.

"Babe, I always have time for you. As a matter of fact, let's go get some lunch."

With that, he stands while still holding me around his waist, and then he gently lets me go so my legs can slide down his muscular thighs. I take in a steadying breath and gradually step back just a little, as I do not want to sever the connection we are sharing. Eventually, there is enough space between us for him to pick up and kiss the back of my hand, which he does before leading me out of the genome room.

As we walked back toward the front of Love It, Own It, we decided to drive separately to a place called Lucile's Bistro. It is one of my favorites in the area. We used to go there every Friday for lunch when I lived on this side of town. He would come pick me up when he finished moonlighting, and we would sit and eat at Lucile's before he had to go home, or he would go to my house to take a nap.

****

Walking into Lucile's feels like visiting your favorite aunt's house. It is comfortable, homey, and familiar. It puts your senses at ease, allowing you to put down the guards and mask you have had to hold in place all day.

We walk through the restaurant until we find our favorite semi-circle booth, which looks freshly remodeled. As we sit down, it still has the same cushy texture, allowing you to melt into your seat while simultaneously allowing the seat to hold you close. We get settled, with us taking opposite sides of the table, where the half-circular table curves around before meeting in the middle. We share a knowing smirk, as we both know these are the spots where the cushion is softest, the food can spread wider, and we can make eye contact from across the table. It is perfect.

As we grin at each other, the waitress comes and takes our orders. The menu has not changed in all this time. It makes the moment we are sharing all the more nostalgic. We order our usual versions of the House Special; this includes a toasted BLT with avocado for me and the same without avocado for him. We also get house-made BBQ chips and a side of fruit. We both ordered a cream soda and a glass of water to drink. After the waitress walks away, we smile at each other.

"So, you done stalling? Or, are you ready to tell me why you were at the store on the floor?" Roe confronts me with a knowing grin.

I smile and shake my head. "I miss your forwardness, Dr. Thibodeaux."

He smirks, "Funny. Actually, I am technically still Dr. Thibodeaux, but I don't practice medicine anymore."

"What?... Come again?" To say I am shocked is beyond an understatement.

"I quit the hospital about four years ago." He smiles.

"You're serious?" I lean forward, because what? This cannot be true.

Snickering, he replies, "Yeah.... why is that so hard to believe?"

"What happened to life visions?"

"Truth is, when you left, I had a lot of soul-searching to do. I realized my life vision didn't include Divine vision. So, I had to make some changes."

"Wow...... Wow." That's all I can say.

As I processed Roe's words, the waitress brought our drinks. After taking a couple of sips, he is back to his original question. "Come on, Shay, what's up? Why am I here?"

"Coincidence." I grin.

"Funny...try again."

Taking a breath, I reply, "Honestly, over the past year and a half, I have made some major changes. I knew I needed to make the changes. However, now, I am not quite sure if what I am doing instead of what I was originally doing is what I am supposed to be doing. Does that make sense?"

"Yes, but you are beating around the bush. Come on. It's me, just spill it."

Before I can respond, the waitress brings our food. I am happy because I need a moment to decide how much I am really going to tell him. I chew slowly, enjoying the familiarity and goodness of the food and thinking. He starts shaking his head after a few minutes.

"What?"

"You are stalling. Speak."

God. I pray silently. God says, "Be completely open with him. That is what he is here for."

I take a grounding breath and explain all the changes I have made. The whole time I am talking, Roe eats and listens. Shaking and nodding his head when appropriate. I continue talking, "So, today I realized enough is enough. Maybe the gurls are right and Antoine is not for me, or maybe I just need a job. Either way, I don't know right now." I finish my statement, slightly exasperated, and take a bite of my sandwich.

He doesn't say anything at first. He takes his time and finishes his sandwich. He just looks up at me from time to time during the process of eating. It is funny because, on the one hand, I should feel like he is not engaging in this conversation, but on the other hand, I realize that he is giving me time to process what I said before he adds his two cents.

I put some chips in my mouth and think about the dreams I have been having. They have been about birds flying to their new destination because of the changing seasons. There is this one pair of birds that are always flying together. They build their nest together. They have baby birds together and set the babies free together. Then, the same pair of birds fly off together again. They are vibrant in color, strong in power, and always together.

When I look up, his eyes sparkle like he knows things I do not. I beam at him. This is how our lunches used to always go. One of us would bring up something profound, and then there would be silence while the person who divulged all their issues ciphered through their thoughts.

I finally take the moment and do what I know I need to do next, which is ask God the question I have avoided asking. I divert my eyes from Roe and pray inwardly, *"God, did I make the right changes to the right places in my life?"* God says, "Yes and no. You needed to leave the company; that phase of your life was over. And you needed to sell your house, but you did not need to move in with Antoine. He is not the one I have for you." I breathe long and deeply, closing my eyes and letting God's words marinate within me. Eventually, I opened my eyes, and they found their way back to Roe, only to find him leaning back and staring at me.

"What?" I question.

"You know, when you dream about birds, it usually means you are ready for the next." There is no smile on his lips as he speaks. He is gentle yet serious. He continues, "Birds mean you can take flight and move into new territory freely. New beginnings and all that...It is cool to have someone there to fly with you as well. To help you take flight, for you guys to lean on each other, support, learn from, and elevate each other. You know?"

I stared at him momentarily, slightly perplexed, as I did not tell him I had been dreaming about birds. However, I should have known I was not the only one dreaming about birds. But then again, we have been estranged for five years. There could have been some spiritual distance during that time.

Before responding to the statements, I know I did not speak out loud, he leaned forward and crossed his arms on the table, then pointed between us and smiled sweetly, saying, "We are spiritually connected, Baby. That means time and space do not matter. Only this does."

I grab his hand and squeeze it. "I missed you." I grin.

He kisses the back of my hand gently. Then I say, "I know, I made some wrong turns. I guess I need to fix that."

"Sounds like a good plan. You need some help?"

"I might." I chuckle.

He scoots over and puts an arm around the back of the booth behind me, "Don't worry. I got you. We fly together, remember."

"Always," I say as I lean into his arms, and he squeezes me close. He kisses that place in front of my ear as only he does, and for a time, we just sit there and watch the other customers. Nothing else needs to be said. The silence is wonderful. It feels good and relaxing to lie in his arms. I could truly stay here forever, feeling safe, protected, and loved... Umm, that is a new thought. Interesting.

Chapter 10 - Monroe

After lunch, we decided to take a walk around the town center that Lucile's now sits in. When Shay and I first started going to Lucile's for lunch, there was nothing else around here but a braid shop, a beauty supply, and a gas station. Now, there is a full town center with a Macy's, Nordstrom Rack, Forever 21, Nike store, Victoria's Secret, etc.... There is something for everyone, including Target and Barnes & Noble.

We walk, browse the shops, and talk. We laugh about old times and the things we used to get into. Then, she takes one of those long breaths, the kind that are heavy with unspoken truths. And that is when I know things are about to get serious again.

She inquires, "So, you told me that you no longer practice medicine and that you have found Divine vision. So, what does that mean?"

I smile slightly, "Well, I opened an art gallery in the Heights. It's called Destined."

She gives me a radiant smile that brightens her entire face, "An art gallery? Really? What artists do you sell?"

"Different ones, depending on who we are showing. Sometimes, there are famous artists, sometimes local artists, and sometimes new artists from around the world. It just depends." I reply as we walk.

"Do you show your paintings?"

"Is that your way of asking if I paint for a living?"

"Yeah, so.....?"

"Yeah, my work is always on display." I grin as she stops walking. I look at her and see the pure elation dancing in her eyes in response to what I just shared.

"You did it!" She exclaims.

"Yeah, I decided to listen to the Divine and do what truly makes me happy. Paint and sculpt." I shrug like it is no big deal, but in truth, she and I both know it is a major life-changing choice and accomplishment.

"I'm so happy for you." She grabs me into a warm, heartfelt hug, and I return the embrace with the same giving energy. "This is so amazing! I will have to come by your spot." She says.

"Please do. Let me know when you are coming, and I will give you a tour."

"Will do." She smirks as she bites her lower lip.

She loops her arm through mine when we release each other from the hug we shared. Then, we continue to walk with her head resting against my arm. It is peaceful and relaxing just to share each other's space. I miss being with someone that I do not need to fill the silence between us with words or anything else, where their presence is enough for me, and mine is enough for them.

As we walk back to our cars, I finally say, "So..."

"Oh no, here you go." She says with a slight groan, but she stays in the same position, resting against me.

"What makes you happy?" I ask gently.

She takes a moment and thinks about my question. That is something else I miss: someone taking the time to think about my questions before just answering them with their first thought. When we reach her SUV, we lean against the driver's side, standing side by side. Some time passes, and I don't rush her. I wait.

When she is ready, she turns to face me with her shoulder leaning against the SUV; she says, "Truly, what makes me happy is peace and joy. I want to live in a place of pure, divine, joyful peace and bring that into the lives of other people." Her face lights up as she continues, "You know, there is a difference between just peace and joyful peace. Peace is quiet and grounding, but it can leave you melancholy. Joyful peace is soothing, grounding, and has joy intermingled into its inner pieces. The latter kind of peace has that unmistakable feeling that everything is good, no matter what it looks like. You know?"

I smile and just nod my head. I don't want to interrupt her flow with my words.

"I want to live knowing that day in and day out, I help make joyful peace happen for people." She looks down, then sighs, "I used to feel something like that with interior design, but then the hustle of running that business took the joy and the peace out of it. Plus, it was like the bigger we got, the less I actually got to design. Then, I didn't even want to be there anymore...... I don't know."

She pauses for a while and looks off into the distance. It is then that I decide to speak. "Baby, when was the last time you felt joyful peace?"

She shrugs. I continue, "Now, you know I ain't taking that as an answer." I bump her shoulder with mine.

"Fine," she states as she rolls her eyes with a smile. "Honestly, like 10 years ago, when you and I went on that vacation to St. Lucia together. I remember sitting on the patio watching you swim in the private pool and thinking this was the life. We had attended that sound bath and prayer session, and everything just felt right."

"What about it was right?"

She smiles nostalgically and looks to the sky with her back resting against her SUV, "Everything."

"What's different now?"

"I think I am trying instead of just being. Just being me, walking in the moments that God has afforded me. You know?" She looks at me.

"Yeah. I get it." It is my turn to look away. I look at my watch and realize that it is getting late. I need to get to the gallery for the showing tonight. "Hey, you want to come to Destined tonight? We are showing a local artist. There will be hors d'oeuvres and wine." I smile. "It starts at 8:00."

"That sounds good.....Oh, but I need to check with my boyfriend, Antoine, about tonight's plan." She winces.

I put my hand on her shoulder. "Bring him. The more the merrier."

"Are you sure? I don't want it to be weird."

"Why would it be weird? We are friends, right?"

"Yeah, but…Do you have a girlfriend?"

"How you gone just slide that in like that?" I laugh.

"Sorry, I just realized we haven't had that conversation yet. So…… do you?"

"No. I don't." I say as I shake my head. She looks at me like I'd better say more, so I continue. "I dated someone for a few months, but it didn't last because, I quote, I have 'commitment issues.'"

She chuckles and says, "No, you don't…. Well, you didn't." She smirks.

I push her slightly. "I don't. I just take my time to make my choice, that's all."

"Is that the story you are telling yourself?"

"No, there are other things I tell myself. However, that is what I tell everyone else."

At this point in the conversation, I am standing in front of her because I need to go. She pushes off the car, walks closer into my space, and says, "And what do you tell your friends? Well, your best friend."

"Is that what we are?"

"Ouch, ok. Am I an associate kind of friend? You did buy me lunch." She laughs.

I walk closer into her space and allow my voice to drop an octave when I say, "You are my best friend, and you have been since the day we met. Time and space do not change that, even if we are not talking."

I can see her take a deep breath and release it. Interesting. My octave change still has the same effect as it did in New Orleans. Noted. After a moment, she says a little more breathy, "Good to know...... So, what is your real answer then?" She gazes up into my face, as I am much taller than she.

I gaze into her eyes from beneath my lashes and feel the energy between us change. It has gone from fun to flirty in seconds. I go with it. Stepping even closer and dropping another octave and tone simultaneously, I say, "I am only interested in being fully committed to one woman who has caramel-colored eyes and happens to be my best friend. So, until she and I can figure that out, I will not be committing fully to anyone."

With that, I inhale the slow, measured exhalation she takes. I lean forward and take her keys from her hand. I click the alarm and move to open her door. She steps to the side, allowing me to open her door fully.

Before she slides in the car, she takes her keys from me and says in a low, sultry voice, "Noted. Mr. Thibodeaux..." We gaze into each other's eyes longer than is appropriate for a pair of best friends. She finally slides into the car, and I close her door.

After starting the engine, she rolls down the window. I step back because everything in me wants to touch her in ways that I should not, yet or not again at the moment. I smile and ask, "Is your number the same? If so, I can text you the address and attire for tonight in case you decide to come."

"Yeah, it's the same. I will see you later, Babes." She winks at me. I shake my head and back away from the car so she can pull off.

I cannot help but laugh as I walk to my Santorini black Jaguar F-type 75 coupe with custom rims. As I get adjusted in my driver's seat, I text LeShay the information for tonight. Then, I start to think about the fact that I may be way over my head with her and this. *Lord, Help.* I pray silently.

Chapter 11 – LeShay

I pull into the garage, thinking I made it home right before Antoine. But before I can say thank God and let down the garage, Antoine is pulling into the driveway in his black BMW 530i. I look at the clock; sure enough, it is five pm on the dot. It's like clockwork. If only I did not need gas to make it home, I would have beaten him. Now, he will want to know where I was and what I did today.

One of the things that I have noticed since I moved in is that Antoine does not ask me how my day was or what I did. It is as if he thinks I sat at home all day waiting for him. I guess that is not that far off from what I have been doing, especially since I have not really gone anywhere over the past few months. All I have been doing is unpacking, and when that was done, there was nothing else for me to do, which is precisely why I went out today. But for some reason, it feels weird to tell him about the fact that I went out today. It's almost like I was doing something I should not have been doing.

Okay, I can be honest with myself. I probably feel that way because some of my conversations with Roe got a little flirtatious. Plus, for the first time, I realized how sexy Roe truly is. I mean, yeah, he is 6'1", but he also has mocha-colored skin and deep, brown, dreamy, almond-shaped eyes. Today, those eyes made me feel like there was hope and a promise of pleasure after all this confusion was figured out.

Over the past five years, Roe has thickened up in the most wonderful of ways. Where he used to be all lean muscle like the swimmer, he now has a little more bulk and definition in his arms and thighs. The way he stood while still holding me in place at the furniture store had my head spinning. His style has even changed from that professional polo and khaki look to a look that includes a button-up shirt with rolled sleeves, dark-washed jeans, and custom Jordans on his feet. He looked like the very grown and sexy version of the man I met at Da Spot all those years ago.

I am forced out of my mental reexamination of Roe by a knock at my window. Right, Antoine just pulled in. I unlock the door, and Antoine opens it. He eyes my attire as I get out of the car, but he says nothing. He just watches me as we enter the house. I put my purse on the counter in the kitchen, and I opened the refrigerator. As I pursue its contents, I can feel Antoine's eyes on me. I do not say anything; I just keep looking for dinner options. After a few minutes, I pull out some fresh veggies to roast in the oven and some chicken to pan-fry. When I turn around, he finally decides to speak.

"So, what did *you* do today?" He asks sarcastically.

Great. The first question he asks is sarcastic, and it is the exact question I don't want to answer. I played it cool and replied, "I went for a drive. I needed to get out of the house.... I was thinking I may need to get a job."

"Why, I make enough money. You can stay home or help a charity."

I instantly stopped washing the vegetables and just looked at him. Is that really what he thinks I want to do? I place my hand on my hip and ask as calmly as I can, "Antoine, where do you see us in the next five years?"

I know I pulled out the big guns with that question, but his continual suggestion that I stay home and that I make this my home makes me wonder. Plus, the things we do every day are kind of like an old married couple. And literally, I have cooked almost every night since moving in here, and I don't even like cooking.

He stares at me and begins questioning me with his eyes, before he responds with, "Well, I want us to be married with a child on the way or already working on our second child. I want you to stay home and care for the kids; that's why I was happy when you left your job. It would have eventually gotten in the way of your time with our kids and with me."

I put down the carrots that are in my hand. "Antoine, you know I plan to work somewhere, right? I am just figuring out where that will be right now."

"Yes, I heard you. I was hoping you would fall in love with not working and let me take care of you."

"I don't want to be taken care of to the point that I cannot do what I love."

"But our kids and I will be what you love. There is no need for anything else. My mother stayed home with me and my three siblings, and that is what I want my wife to do, too."

"You have never said any of this."

"Well, I figured we would get to it."

"What if that is not what I want?"

"You don't know what you want. I will help you figure it out." He comes to hug me from behind. "I got you, Baby."

I shrug him off and remove myself from his embrace. "I told you not to call me that." I feel weirded out whenever he calls me Baby.

Anyway, right now, he is not just weirding me out with the nickname; he sounds crazy. Has he forgotten who I am? As I stare at him, I realize he hasn't forgotten. I have. I am the one who does not know what is next, and I have allowed this man to make me think living here with him is a good idea. This conversation makes it very clear that we want different things in life.

To top off what is already happening, he walks closer to me and eyes my outfit. Then, he disapprovingly says, "What's with the dress and eye shadow today? You know I don't like all of that showy stuff."

Excuse me. At this point, both of my hands make their way to my hips as I cock my head to the side, "I was not with you."

"Good point, who were you with?" He is getting testy. I don't think I have ever seen him this way before.

"Myself. I thought I looked good, so I went with it." I feel my neck roll slightly. This is not good.

"Did you need to put your boobs out like that? It looks like you were showcasing to everyone that you are available.

Plus, why did you wait until I was set to arrive home to come back from wherever you went? You should have been home at least an hour ago so that dinner could be ready when I arrived."

Oh yeah, he has lost his whole mind. Shoot, maybe I have, too, because what was I thinking? Yeah, it is time to put some things in order and make some changes. Therefore, I respond, "First of all, my boobs can be wherever I would like them to be. Second, I never said I was making you dinner every night. We could order almost every day for all I care."

"Is that right?" He is mad now. I do not usually talk to him with this much boss in my voice, but he is trippin'. He stands to his full 5'9" frame and walks into my face. It is then that I see the streak of pure evil that flashes behind his eyes. In my spirit, I know it is time to go. Period.

He says, "You will do what I want. So, let's just do that. I am going to shower." With that, he walks off.

Everything in me is telling me to get my purse and leave, so that is exactly what I do. I will have to come get my stuff another day. The look I just saw come across his eyes is one I never want to see again. Which also means he is definitely not someone I should share myself with ever again. Then I hear God say, "He is not for you." I pray in return. *God, I hear you loud and clear.*

Chapter 12 – LeShay

I get in my SUV and start driving. I don't know where I am going. To be honest, I legitimately just left everything right where it was. I am sure that when Antoine comes out, I will get a call. That was the weirdest exchange we have ever had, but one thing my mom always says is, "When someone shows you who they are, believe them." I think she got that from Maya Angelou, but the truth is the truth.

Before I moved in, Antoine was always pleasant and considerate, but like his talking, that went out of the window once I moved in. Don't get me wrong. He is not mean to me. He is just not as affectionate as before. As I am reflecting on this thought, my phone rings. My SUV announces that Antoine is calling. I accept the call to get it over with.

"Hello."

"Where are you?" He says with more force than usual. What is going on with him tonight? The tones and the look in his eyes tonight are like I don't even know this dude, and we have been together for over a year.

"I left."

"To where? We are supposed to have dinner, which is not made, and you and I are to sit and watch TV after. It's my time now." He says with finality.

I pull my car into a Kroger's parking lot because, truly, he has lost his mind. Who does he think he is talking to? Then I hear God say, "You, Beloved. You." I let that marinate. What have I done that made Antoine think this was okay? Shoot, now I sound like a victim. This is done. I'm done.

"Look, Antoine. I don't know what your problem is tonight, but what we are not doing is this. I am not the kind of woman you manage or handle. I am not the kind of woman who stays home, waits for you all day, and cooks dinner every night. I am not that kind of woman..."

"Obviously, because you went out looking like a thot with your breast all out." He interrupts me.

I feel myself as I begin nodding my head. Now, I get it. I say, "So, that is the issue. I left the house, and I left with a little cleavage on display. You know what? I can do whatever I want to do. When you met me, there was a little cleavage on display, and we were at a business dinner."

"Exactly, I have been meaning to tell you that it was time to stop showing my goods."

"Wow...... Your goods.... Got it." I'm nodding again.

"Good, now come home so we can eat and forget this happened. Better yet, we can have make-up sex. We have never done that before. I hear it's amazing."

This dude is crazy. "Antoine, this is not working. We are not working..." I begin.

"What do you mean, we just agreed?"

"No, we didn't. I said, 'Got it,' which meant you have lost your mind. I do not belong to you, and if this is how you treat the woman who does belong to you, I don't want to be her. Look..."

"No, you look. Maybe we got a little heated, and I am sorry. Sweetheart, please come home." And there goes the Antoine I know. The problem is, now, I know the truth, and like the Bible says, the truth will set you free.

"Thank you for the apology, but I cannot be in a relationship with you anymore. We clearly do not want the same things, and moving in together made that fact very obvious. I will send movers to get my things and drop off your keys. Have a great life, Antoine."

"So, that is it. At the first bump in the road, you quit. Is that why you really left your job, because you could not handle it when things got tough?"

Oh yeah, God. I hear you loud and clear. This man is not for me. I don't even know how I missed it. I take a breath, so I don't say the real things going through my mind. Instead, I say, "Antoine, have a great life. Bye." With that, I hang up the phone.

Wow is all I can think. Wow.

I put my car in reverse and back out of the parking space; I have no idea where I am going, but back to that house is not it.

Chapter 13 – LeShay

I find myself driving toward downtown Houston. I decided I should talk to someone, so I called my mom. My mom is what she calls my ace in the pocket. She always has my back and comes through with great advice.

"Hey, Ma. What are you up to?" I say into the car phone.

"Hey, Pumpkin. I am helping your Father find his bowling shoes. I don't know why he won't just put them back in his bowling bag after they air out each week. Mark, did you look by the washing machine?" She yells out to him.

I hear him respond, "See, that's why I asked you. Baby, you always know." I listen as he comes up to her, and they start kissing.

I yell through the phone, "Hey, NASTY!! Daughter on the phone here."

I hear them both laugh. My Pop takes the phone, "Sorry, Sugar Plum, I didn't know you were on the phone. Shaylin, why didn't you tell me?" He asks my mom.

She responds, "Well, you start threatening me with a good time. Shay, you understand, right?"

"Unfortunately, I do. I will talk to y'all later."

"Wait, you don't have to go, Pumpkin. Mark is about to leave."

Pop responds, "Well, I was kind of thinking..."

"Eww, guys. Seriously. Bye. Love you."

They both laugh again and say, "Bye."

We all hang up, and I cannot help but laugh at my parents. They have been married for 30 years, and they still can't get enough of each other. As gross as it is sometimes, as a woman, I can appreciate the way they love each other in a way I didn't quite understand when I was younger.

I take a breath. What now? I could call my gurls, but they are just going to want to go party and celebrate the end of my relationship. I am not ready for that yet. So, instead, I kept driving and ended up in front of The Majestic Hotel near downtown Houston. Deciding to stay there for the night, I pull into the valet and give them my keys.

This hotel looks like the rest of the buildings in downtown as it is made to blend into the towers that make up downtown's skyline. But when you walk into the hotel, the entire vibe changes. Instead of looking like a business hotel with its professional colors and décor, I am greeted with a modern lounge vibe. It is almost like the designer wanted you to feel like you walked into a nightclub intended to help you unwind and relax instead of turning up and getting lit. It is precisely the feeling I need at the moment, so I am excited to see more, especially the rooms.

Once I made it to the reservation desk, I discovered I was in luck, as they had a room available for the next few nights.

I go through the reservation process and get a key for my room. Before too long, I was in the sleek, dark gray-colored, mirrored ceiling elevator. Once I get to my floor, I get off the elevator and am greeted by a hall with doors of different colors. The doors alternate between black, gray, and royal purple. The hall and walls are black with a slightly shimmery coat of paint. The hall carpet is deep gray with a black path down the middle. I take in the large mirrors hanging sporadically down the hall. It is almost like the person looking into the mirror is the artwork. The music that is playing is sensual R&B, and it is at just the right volume level so that you hear it but don't get engulfed in it. It all makes you feel like you are the VIP at a specialty lounge or the special guest at a luxury spa. So much so, I don't know if I want a drink or to chill and have a massage. I am truly digging this vibe.

The other thing I notice as I walk down the hall is that the rooms are nicely spaced. There are only about 12 rooms on this floor. My room number is 512, which happens to be at the end of the hall. When I walk up to the door, my door is royal purple. When I get closer, I notice that it has a slightly shimmery coat to it as well. Interesting.

I put the black key with silver writing against the door's card reader, and the door unlocks. When I walk into the room, the lights appear, casting the room in low mood-setting light. The curtains open to the beautiful downtown skyline, as this hotel sits right on the edge of downtown.

As I walk further into the room, I see a kitchenette. It is complete with a small stove and fridge. The kitchenette is slightly closed off from the small living space by a half wall. The half wall has two parts. One part runs parallel to the entrance to the kitchenette, and the other part runs in front of the kitchenette, leaving it open to the small living space. The part of the wall in front of the kitchenette houses a bar complete with stools for eating. Approaching the living space, I see a black leather sofa with a glass coffee table and a custom stand beneath it. The stand appears to be made of black and gray marble. The floor is dark gray, like the hall. The walls are light gray, and there is an accent wall that is black and purple. It is on the accent wall that I find the mounted TV, which has 'Welcome, Ms. LeShay Fontenot' on the screen. There is a table beneath the TV with fresh candles and a lighter. Interesting.

The living space has a floor-to-ceiling window and presents a gorgeous view before me. Next to the sofa, there is another purple door. I open the door and find the bedroom. The bedroom is a nice contrast to the vibe in the other part of the suite. The walls in the bedroom are light gray, and on the wall housing the bed, there is a lovely swirl design made of purple and dark gray. It is like a painting. As I look closer, I see that there are words painted into the design, "Let Love Lead You, and You Will Fly. Be Free." I smile because the words warm my heart. They are written elegantly above the dark gray headboard of the bed.

The headboard has a cushioned high back so that you can sit up and lean against it. The comforter on the bed is dark gray, almost like the headboard, with a custom swirl that looks just like the one on the wall. The only difference is that the comforter has the swirl in light gray and purple instead of dark gray.

When I turn to my left, I find another floor-to-ceiling window. The view is just as spectacular as the living space. In the bedroom, there is a purple chaise that sits in front of the window. The purple on the chaise matches the purple on the wall and in the comforter. I turn back around and see another purple door.

This door leads to a beautiful black and light gray bathroom. There are light gray walls with a dark purple light lining the walls in the entire bathroom. It cast the bathroom in a calming purple haze. The sink and wall-length counter are custom marble carved into a wavelike shape. In the far corner of the counter, there are two complete dark purple towel sets rolled into a nice display. There is also lavender and honey hand soap and lotion near the sink. There is a beautiful, large heart-shaped mirror above the sink, and at the top of the mirror, in a feminine script, it reads, 'Love Wins Every Time.' I smile at this quote as well.

Walking further into the bathroom, I find that there is a custom black toilet with a black marble toilet paper holder. The toilet is closed in its own mini room, which is complete with a black door. When I turn to the opposite side, another purple door leads to a walk-in closet complete with a floor mirror with a wave-like design framing the entire mirror. In the nook of the closet, I find extra towels, sheets, a blanket, and a pillow on the shelf. I also find the hotel room's complimentary plush black and gray robe and slippers.

When I exit the closet, I finally explore the large jacuzzi tub. On the edge of the tub, there is a welcome basket. The basket contains a card that says, "Hello, Ms. Fontenot; thank you for choosing to stay with us. As our token of appreciation, we would like to offer you this basket of bath goodies. Contained within the basket are cashmere-scented bubble bath, body wash, and lotion. There is also a body scrub and a bath bomb for your soaking pleasure. When you have completed your bath, please look within your suite fridge and find a chilled bottle of wine and chocolate-covered strawberries. Again, thank you for visiting us, and we hope to see you again real soon."

I open the basket, and the cashmere scent that fills the space is perfect. It is slightly sweet with a hint of lilies and a hint of mahogany. I think I might just indulge in a bath tonight. After all, the entire suite gives a vibe that is grounding and reflective. A bath would be the perfect place to do that.

As I consider this, I explore the standing shower, which is complete with medium gray tile and three shower heads. There are shampoo, conditioner, and body wash dispensers in the shower that contain the same lavender and honey scent as the hand soap. The shower looks like a dream, ready to soothe your troubles away.

The interior designer for this hotel did their thang. This place is fantastic, and every detail encourages and enhances the grown and sexy chill vibe that started at the hotel entrance while allowing you to feel grounded in space. This hotel is definitely a gem to find are my thoughts as I returned to the suite's main door and put out the do not disturb sign.

I lock the extra lock and admit to myself that it is not lost on me that this hotel room has the same color and shimmered door as the purple door that plagued dreams so many years ago. I choose not to dwell on that fact as I do not believe in coincidences, but I am not in the right mental space to deal with the meaning at this moment. Maybe another day, just not right now.

With that, I walk back to the closet and place my purse on one of the shelves of the closet's nook. I also remove my clothes and hang them in the closet. Then I run myself a bubble bath and top it off with a bath bomb. The cashmere scent further saturates the space, as the bath bomb melts into the water. The steam that begins to fill the room, along with the calming scent of cashmere, begins to relax my mind and spirit just as I step into the warm, slightly hot bath water, which instantly soothes the tension in my body.

I lean back and start the jacuzzi jets, allowing the jets to work out the kinks of my muscles. I lay my head back and think, Wow, how things have changed. Who would have thought that Antoine would turn out to be the dude he was tonight? *Thank you, God, for showing me now. So that I didn't go too far,* I prayed silently.

The question is, now what? I don't have a place to stay. Yes, I could go home to my parents' house, but that is not a real option I want to take. I don't have a job. If I am honest, I want a job. I am just not sure what kind of job I want at this point.

With these thoughts going through my mind, I decided to pick up my phone, which is sitting on the floor next to the tub, and go to my Chill playlist. Once I find it, I press play. All of my thoughts need answers, but I don't have to answer them right now, not today. So, I let my thoughts flow without interacting with them until they eventually stop coming, and mental silence takes their place. It is then that I can finally chill, finally relax.

After about 30 minutes, I get out of the bath and shower. As I finish putting on the creamy whipped lotion from the bath basket, my phone beeps. It is a text from Monroe. Oh shoot, I completely forgot about the event tonight. I open the text.

So that is what we doin dis go round? Not showing up.

Im so sorry. Things got a little crazy when I got hm.

Everything ok?

Umm yes and no.

What does that mean?

How was the event?

No, try again. Are you ok?

I cannot lie to Roe, so I texted, **I will be**

Where are you?

How was the event?

It was fine. Sold a few pieces. The artist is still lookin for his voice. Ur turn where r u?

At a hotel

I see the three dots flashing, but no text message comes through; instead, I am getting a call. I accepted the call as I went to get the hotel robe and slippers to put on.

I answer sweetly, "Hello, Baby."

"Hey, what cha mean you're at a hotel?" Roe responds in that straightforward way of his.

"You know, it is 2 am, right?" I ask as I put on the robe and walk to the kitchenette.

"Yeah, I didn't expect you to answer my text until later this morning."

"So, why send it?"

"Because I am filing away the last of the payments from tonight, and I didn't want to forget." With a frustrated sigh, he continues, "Your turn."

"So, bossy."

"Stop stalling. Baby, are you ok?"

"Physically, yes…… Look, basically, my boyfriend did a Dr. Jeckel and Mr. Hyde on me."

"He put his hands on you?" I can hear the anger rise almost instantaneously. Interesting.

Calmly, I state, "No. It was just in his eyes and the tone of his voice. He got mad because I was out today, and I had a little cleavage on display." I state as I take the delicious-looking chocolate-covered strawberries out of the fridge and place them on the counter. I also take out the bottle of pink champagne and almost jump for joy. It is my favorite brand and the only champagne I drink. Yay me!

I start to look for a wine bottle opener. Then I realized there had been a long pause on the other end of the call. "Roe?"

"Well, I mean, there was more than a little cleavage out there on display." I can hear the smile in his voice.

"I'm sorry. Was there something wrong with my dress?" I question as I find the wine opener and uncork the wine.

"No, you looked beautiful today."

"Thank you." I pour some wine into one of the crystal wine glasses from the cabinet.

"So, you're at a hotel…. What happened?"

"I straight walked out when he was in the shower. Everything within me was like, leave, go now. So, here I am." I shrug like he can see me. I pick up the tray of strawberries, grab my very full glass of champagne, and put both of them on the coffee table in front of the sofa.

"That's wild…. Wait, but y'all lived together, right?"

I take a seat on the firm but soft sofa. As soon as I sit, it is as if the sofa curves to my body. A moan leaves my lips before I can stop it.

"Umm. Should I go?" Roe asks suspiciously.

"No, sorry." I laugh out of embarrassment. "I just sat on this sofa, and it feels so amazing. It's like it just hugged me." I grab my wine and settle deeper into the sofa.

"That sounds amazing." I hear him set an alarm and start walking. "Where are you staying?"

"That new hotel on the edge of downtown, The Majestic Hotel. It is really nice. They even left a bath basket and chocolate-covered strawberries. And, get this, they have that rare pink champagne I like. You know, the one we found in Napa Valley at that wine festival."

"Really…. Yeah, I remember it's called……"

"Château de Amour." We say in unison, and we laugh together.

I take a sip of my wine and hum in satisfaction. It is slightly sweet with hints of butter. It is so good.

"You just took a sip, huh?" He inquires.

"I did. Oh, my Gaud. How I miss this wine." I lean my head back.

"Has it been that long since you had a glass?" He is now in his car, driving.

"Yeah, you know I usually only drink this when I am celebrating or truly treating myself. This bottle ain't cheap by any means."

"True. You had me buy it enough time for me to remember."

"Funny." I take another sip. I put the phone on speaker and take a bite of one of the strawberries. Another moan leaves my mouth instantly.

"Baby, you can't be making those sounds while you are on the phone with me." He states with a little strain in his voice.

"Sorry, these strawberries are so delicious. They are sweet and juicy..." I take another bite and do my best to muffle another moan. I hear him chuckle. "Roe, for real, and this chocolate. Oh, my Gaud. I may just live here." I settle back into the sofa.

"That's the plan, then?"

"Maybe. For the first time in my life, there is no plan for my next. None at all." I lift my wine glass in a toast to myself.

"Maybe you should go to the spa tomorrow and indulge in a few services."

"You say that like you have been to this spa before."

"I have."

I wait for him to say more, but he doesn't. "Roe, you can't just say that, and that's it."

"Actually, I can..." He is smiling, I can tell.

"Roe?"

"Look, the spa there is great. How about I pay for you to go to the spa tomorrow? I will pick out some things I know you will like, and when you are done, we can have dinner."

"That actually sounds really nice. You know I don't need you to..."

"Shay, let me take care of you. Today has been a lot, I am sure."

Oh, how I miss this man. Sighing, I say, "Ok, but don't make the reservation too early. I need to set up the movers and get some clothes delivered."

"Ok. I will send you the reservation once I have it booked." I hear him get out of his car and let down the garage. I hear the door open and close to what I assume is his house, and then the sound of an alarm disarming.

"Roe?" I can hear that the tone in my voice has gotten a little sultrier due to the second and third things I love about this wine. It is laced with CBD and has a really nice alcohol content. I am feeling good already.

"Shay, you are tipsy already, Baby." The rhythm of his voice has slowed down, and there is a little more bass than a second ago.

"Sounds that way, huh?"

"I should go."

"Why? We are talking."

"Shay, we are friends, right?"

"Yeah."

"So, I will be honest. Between the moaning, to you talking about sweet and juicy strawberries, to the tone of your voice now, I am thinking about things that friends shouldn't. So, I am going to go, then make your reservation, and I will see you tomorrow. Ok?"

"Are you going to take a cold shower?"

"See, there you go. Bye, Baby."

"Wait."

"What?" He says with restrained frustration. I want to laugh, but I also want to know what he is thinking. I am playing with fire, and I know it.

On second thought, I decided to stop fanning the flames this time. This time, really? Interesting, I say to myself. However, to him, I say, "Thank you for calling and wanting to take care of me. And thank you for today. I had a great time hanging out with you. I really miss this, us. Sorry, I messed that up."

"You are welcome, but you never have to thank me for any of that. I got you. Plus, we both messed this, us, up. So, let's get back on the right page—no more apologies about stuff from our past. Let's move forward. Ok?"

"Ok."

"I'm going to go. Sleep well, Baby."

"You too."

With that, we hang up, and I eat the rest of the strawberries and finish my glass of wine. Then, I fall into a blissful sleep on the sofa as it hugs me close.

Chapter 14 – Monroe

Walking through the garden, I smell the lilies and roses. As I examine their beauty, I see they are an array of purple, red, and white. As I walk, I can feel the sun's rays gazing onto my bare back, just as I can feel the soft grass hugging gently around my toes. I saunter through the V-shape of the garden until I get to the gray and black fountain, which sits at the apex of the garden. Standing in front of the fountain, I see that the fountain is made of a sculptured carving of a woman and a man holding each other in a lover's embrace. The technique the artist used to sculpt the fountain is amazing and breathtaking. The fountain is smooth, and there are no jagged pieces. You can feel the artist's love for the other person in the sculpture. As I admire the craftsmanship, I walk around the fountain, and at the bottom, there is the artist's signature. Dipping down so I can see clearly. I see in a familiar carved script M. Marquis T.

Running my hand across the signature that is mine, I feel the soothing presence of God all around me. Then I hear footsteps, slow, steady, and soft against the grass. I turn toward the sound and see my wife approaching me. I don't know how I know she is mine, but she is, I am sure of it. I cannot see her face, but I know it is her. When she reaches me, I stand and pull her close as she removes her wide-rim hat. I take in the beauty of her face. The face of the woman I have loved since the first time I held her in my arms in the back of my car at the drive-in movie.

As I look into LeShay's beautiful face, I am held captive by the love and clarity in her eyes. I allow my eyes to linger on her smile. It is a smile of complete joy and contentment. A smile of joyful peace. I pick her up and she wraps her arms and legs around me as I walk us back to our house. As I walk, she gives me sweet kisses on my cheeks and then whispers, "I love you, Bae."

With that image and feeling in mind, I wake up from my blissful dream. I open my eyes and smile. Of course, I still dream about the house and the purple door. I still dream about Shay and the kids. It is just not as often as it was some years ago. It is almost like I needed to know where I was going to help me make the changes necessary to get there.

I stretch my arms above my head, allowing my custom mattress to mold to my body. My deep blue satin sheets feel good against my skin, as I tend to sleep in the nude. I fold my arms behind my head and enjoy the view of my garden from my bedroom bay window, whose middle window is a patio door with floor-to-ceiling folding glass doors. When I built this house, I completed the pool, and it sits right behind the living room, but on the other side of the expansive backyard, it was empty, just grass. Then, I started dreaming about gardens with different types of flowers until one day, there was a V-shaped garden in the back of my house with lilies and roses. After that dream, I started working to build the garden I can now see from my bed. Last night was the first night I dreamt about the actual end of the garden. The statue/fountain in the dream was impressive. I actually just bought some of the material needed for the fountain from my distributor out of state. It should be here either today or tomorrow.

The thought of making the sculpture from my dream has me feeling excited and ready for my day. Since it is Saturday, I don't have much to do but go to the bank and make a deposit. I think I will also stop by a store or two to pick up tools and a base for this fountain. The artist in me is awake and ready to create.

When I sit up and swing my legs to the side of the bed, I remember what Shay said in my dream, "I love you, Bae." In all the dreams I have had about us over the years, she has never called me Bae in that tone before. It was a tone of unconditional love, adoration, completeness, and vastness of heart.

It makes me think about when we started calling each other Baby. She told me I could call her anything but Bae because that nickname was for her man only. At the time, I was like, Cool, no problem, because I wasn't her man. But now, I would love to be.

As I think about that conversation, I start my hygiene routine to prepare for the rest of the day. As I get dressed, thoughts of Shay fill my mind. It is wild that she and her dude broke up right when we reconnected. Then again, maybe it is not unbelievable at all; perhaps it is divine providence.

I brush my shoulder-length hair into a ponytail and then decide to put on my navy blue beanie to match my lightweight long-sleeve navy blue shirt with a white strip. I also have on dark blue jeans and some deep royal blue Air Jordan 12s. With my hair nicely tucked and my beard and mustache brushed just right, I spray on my custom cologne, and I am ready to go.

****

It is about 4pm at this point, and I am in the Art Décor shop trying to find the perfect base for this fountain. I could make the base, but since it is a fountain, I would like to purchase the base to ensure that it is secure and can hold the water of the fountain while protecting the material that the fountain is made of. As I walk down the aisle and think about making the base myself because I am not finding what I want, my phone starts to ring. Knowing the ringtone, I answered the call with my AirPod Pros, already in my ears.

"What's up, Christo? How you hangin?" I greet my big brother.

"Hey, Roe. I'm good, just working and moving."

"You always working, Sto."

"Whatever, so are you. You probably buying art supplies right now."

I laugh, "Fair enough, but my work and my hobby are the same thing, at this point."

"Touché. Touché." We laugh.

"So, what's up? This is not our normal lunch on Monday check-in call. Everything good?" I ask as I pick up material to make the base I want, along with some other things I will need.

"Mom would like us all to come home and meet her boyfriend." He states plainly.

I stop walking, "I'm sorry. Come again?"

"You heard what I said."

I start walking again, "She never introduces us. Has Marcus met him?"

"Nope."

"Wow, so she is really into this dude?"

"Looks that way, Roe. Get this, she won't even give me his first name."

I start laughing, "Cause she knows you are going to do a full background check and produce a whole genogram on the dude's family."

"And?"

"Sto, that is not normal. Regular people do a Google and social media search. Not have a full CIA background check and stakeout on the guy."

"I don't know what you mean. The CIA does not work on domestic issues."

"Ok. But last time you said, and I quote, 'Ma's house sits on Shelia Island, that is foreign soil with its own government,'"

"We got what we needed, did we not?" He states seriously.

"Christo, for real, should we be worried?"

"I don't know. I think she is serious about this one. She has never formally had a dinner gathering to introduce us to her boyfriend. I think we should be prepared for anything."

"What kind of dinner is this, and when?"

"The kind where she said dress nice and bring our 'lady friends.' She wants us to confirm we can come for Thanksgiving."

"Thanksgiving? And bring a lady friend? If we have a friend to bring to Thanksgiving, we must also be serious about said friend."

"Exactly. I think she is also trying to figure out what we are up to. You know how she do."

"True." I pick out the last few items I need and look at my watch. I need to get out of here.

"So, Roe, you gonna be there, right?"

"Stop acting like I have a choice. Yes, I will see y'all in about a month."

"Alright, got to go. Duty calls. Stay safe."

"You too, Sto."

After hanging up, I get in line to check out.

****

Check-out takes about 15 minutes. By the time I have changed into my navy-blue tailored button-down shirt complete with initials on the cuff, which have been rolled to quarter-length sleeves, straightened my beanie, and sprayed on some more cologne, all in the car by the way, it is now about 5:30 p.m. This means I can head to pick up Shay.

When I texted her the confirmation last night, there was a spa reservation that should have kept her at the spa until 4 p.m., and then I said I would pick her up at the valet at 6 p.m.

I pull up to the valet at 5:58 p.m. This gives me the marvelous opportunity to see LeShay walk out of the hotel in a long-sleeve, short, body-hugging Balmain dress, complete with a Marc Jacobs camera bag and some Louboutin booties. Her locs are crinkly and hang beautifully against her body. I step out of the car and walk around. That is when I explore her gorgeous face with my eyes. She has a slight smoky eye with a red lip. She looks absolutely stunning. The most captivating part is the clarity and love in her eyes. It is the exact look I saw in my dream last night.

Umm, tonight is definitely about to be interesting.

Chapter 15 – LeShay

When Monroe hugs me, it is slow and luxurious. He smells phenomenal. I hug him close, and then I step back as he opens the car door for me. As I slide into his black Jag, the skirt of my mid-thigh dress rises higher. I hear his sharp intake of breath as I settle into place. I smirk.

He gets into the driver's seat, and we pull off. The soft leather of his car's seat holds me close, making me feel like someone is caressing my thighs as Roe takes every turn. We have not said anything, and I can see him grabbing and releasing the steering wheel. This tells me he is processing what he wants to say. Within 10 minutes, we pull into a luxury restaurant called Fire & Desire. It specializes in romantic dinners and award-winning desserts. I have been dying to come here since they opened, but Antoine thought it was too expensive. The valet opens my door and helps me out. Roe comes around and takes my hand in his.

As we walk into the restaurant, I take in the deep maroon, shimmery silver, and dark gray that make up the décor. The interior designer did a fantastic job of ensuring the walls within the restaurant provide each table privacy while allowing the entire space to still feel unobstructed. There is a nice balance of openness and mystery. Roe made a reservation because, before long, we were being led to our seats. As we were guided to our booth, I noticed the booths are made into different shapes. They are either a heart, a flower of some sort, or lip-shaped.

Each booth is dark maroon and has a candle providing just the right amount of light for the patron's table. There is enough light to see your food and the face of the one you are with, but also enough shadow to add a sensual, sexy vibe to your dinner. Our booth is at the back of the restaurant. As we approach the back, I realize that what I thought was a back accent wall is individually enclosed tables facing the manufactured lake with a fountain located in the back of the restaurant. I know the lake's location, as we saw the lake when we were driving into the valet area. Unlike the other booths in the restaurant, these booths are completely shielded on the sides and the back. No one can see in except for the people sitting at their individual tables.

Before we can enter the back section, there is a card reader. As the hostess places her badge against the reader, she turns to us and says, "Welcome to the VIP Corner. Only guests sitting in this area and the waiters serving them are allowed in this section." She walks us to the far corner and says, "This is your table. It is the rose table. She scans her card again, and a door opens to the enclosed, private dining space. She motions for us to enter. Monroe allows me to go in first.

Our booth is shaped like a rose. It is a deep maroon like the tables in the other section, but it is shaped like a circular loveseat with unique armrests. The table itself is made of custom ebony wood and is shaped like the root of a tree. The design is elaborate and beautiful. You can see the different shadows of the wood and where it was cut and sanded. The table is smooth to the touch as I run my hand across it to get to the other side of the booth. We have a candle burning that smells like warm vanilla and musk. It is sweet and sensual. The table has silverware wrapped in dark gray and held together by a shimmery rose-shaped napkin ring.

Monroe settles into the booth next to me, and the smell of the candle mixed with his custom apple cedarwood cologne makes for a heady aroma. Right now, he is sitting about a foot away from me. It is close enough to be fully aware of him, but not touching him.

After we are settled, the hostess explains that per the reservation requirements, we will be having the Chef's Choice tonight. She describes the different dishes that will make up our four-course meal. It all sounds absolutely delicious. She lets us know that when we are ready for our next course, we just need to press the small lit button next to the armrest near the door, which is on Monroe's side for us. She lets us know that we would not be interrupted or visited by the waiter after the first time until the button was pressed again. This practice ensured our privacy during our private dining experience. She then asked if we had any questions, but we didn't. So, she gracefully took her leave.

Almost immediately, our waiter arrives with our first course. He reiterates about the button, and then we are left alone. Monroe prays for our food, and then we start the appetizer, a delectable seafood fondue with crab, shrimp, and cheese served with homemade bread and homemade pita chips. After we plate our appetizer, we slowly lift our heads and look at each other. We smile and take the first bite simultaneously, the way we used to.

We used to like going out to try out new restaurants and different varieties of food. We would always take the first bite of each dish together, so we both had a new experience harmoniously. Then, we would talk about it.

As soon as the yummy cheese of the fondue touches my tongue, I moan. Then, I hear Roe do the same thing. I look at him and see that he is looking at his chip like, damn. I snicker, and he gazes my way with a wink.

"This is so good." He moans as he takes another bite. The deep rumble of his moan reminds me of the things I thought about during my spa visit today.

I stare at him for a second before taking another bite.

After a few more bites, he says, "Shay, I am sorry about how sensual this atmosphere is. I knew it was said to be romantic. But I didn't realize it was like this."

"Don't worry, Baby. I have been dying to come here. The aesthetics are amazing, and this food is delicious so far. So, no worries." I respond while smiling sweetly.

Slowly, we enjoy each bite of our appetizer, and when we are finished, we call for the salad. The salad is a mixed greens salad with almonds, olives, tomatoes, shredded parmesan, and cucumbers. A handmade specialty dressing combines it all into a tasty melody of flavors. We both moan on the first bite. We shake our heads at each other. This food is tremendously delectable.

At this point, we are not conversing, and the air between us is thick with all the unspoken things we have yet to say. When I finish my salad, I push it to the side. Roe moves to press the button, but I place my hand slightly on his arm to stop him. He looks at me.

"Can we talk for a minute?" I ask.

"Am I in trouble?" He inquires.

"No." I smile.

With that, he settles back on his side of the booth and angles toward me so that we are facing each other. He removes his beanie and runs his hands through his curly mane, undoing the ponytail beneath and placing his hair tie in his pocket. I love his hair; he knows how I love running my fingers through it. He replaces his beanie, winks at me, and leans back, waiting for me.

I start, "First, let me say, thank you for the spa this afternoon. It was truly extraordinary and mesmerizing; everything was incredibly on point, from the body scrub to the milk bath to the hot stone massage to the facial. When the lady came in to give me a sound bath during the milk bath, I almost lost my mind." I grin.

He smiles, "Yeah, I thought you would like that."

"Yeah, it was thoughtful and so needed. I felt cared for and rejuvenated."

"My pleasure." He replies in that deep octave he gets when he is relaxed.

I lean back and then say, "While I lay on the chaise in the oxygen room, which, by the way, was unbelievable. I decided to do some real soul-searching......You know that I don't do well, not knowing what to do, especially when I should know. You know?"

"Yeah, but are you supposed to know right now?" He questions with an arched eyebrow.

"Truth?"

"Always." He smirks.

Sighing and smiling in return, I decide to be transparent. "It has been time for me to know for a few years. I have been running because I was uncertain of what life would be like when I did know. I wasn't sure how life would change. However, I am tired of running and tired of trying to figure things out, especially when the Creator and I could just talk about it.......So...... today, in the oxygen room, I finally, truly just asked what is supposed to happen in my life from here, where am I supposed to be in life and in my relationships...."

I look at my hands and then out of the window before us. I question if I am ready to share what I am about to say with anyone. However, if I am going to share with someone, Roe is the only one I would share it with at this point. So, I guess here goes.

Looking back at Monroe, he is waiting for me. One of the marvelous things about having a conversation with Roe is that he understands that silence during a conversation is not always ominous. He, like me, allows people to have the moment they need before they continue. This is precisely what he is doing right now, giving me time to collect my thoughts so that I can say what I need to say.

He is observing me, taking in my facial expressions and non-verbal communication. For instance, he must realize that I am nervous because he takes my hand resting on the table and kisses the back of it. Then, he squeezes it slightly. He intertwines our fingers and sits just holding hands with me for a minute.

After I took another few deep breaths, I continued, "I wasn't wrong in choosing interior design, but I was wrong in where I did it. I wasn't wrong in wanting more in a relationship; I was just wrong with whom. After talking it over with God, I understand that I should open another interior design business; however, it should specialize in spiritual places like spiritual wellness and healing businesses and churches. I want to design the best place for people to connect with themselves and with God so they can fully grow into the wonderful people they were created to be. I would even be willing to design private suites or rooms in residential properties or businesses that want to add a meditation or reiki room to their homes or companies." I see the excitement brewing in his eyes. I continued, "I want to have consultation interviews, and once a contract is signed, I want to perform Reiki and meditate with the person I will design for. This will allow me and the person to be on the same spiritual page and ensure I can best serve them in the capacity they need." I take a breath and gaze into his eyes. His face is lit up with pure elation.

I take a long exhale to release the rest of the nervous energy that came with sharing the divine vision God had given me, and then I ask, "What do you think?"

He scoots closer to me and kisses the back of my hand again, "Baby, that sounds awesome."

"Yeah? You don't think it's too out of the box for me?"

"No," he quickly responds and continues with, "Plus, if God said to do it, it will be great. You got this! I am so proud and happy for you."

"Thank you," I reply with a sense of relief. I lean in, and we share a nice, friendly hug. After a moment or two, He leans back and presses the button for our next course.

"Before you continue, can I say something?" He asks.

"Of course."

"Baby, you look deliciously gorgeous tonight."

"Yeah?"

"Absolutely…. I'm sorry it took me so long to say it. I was trying to find the *best friend* way to say it, but, yeah…." He responds with a shrug of his shoulders.

"Well, delicious is not quite the adjective for a friend…" I grin as the waiter comes in and brings our Bone-In Rib-Eye Steaks with green beans and garlic mashed potatoes as our sides.

Talking completely ceases as we cut into our steaks. They are cooked to perfection, with Roe's having that thin layer of pink with a crispy outside and dripping in a special steak sauce, and mine being well done but still juicy with a parmesan crust topper.

The waiter takes his leave after refilling our water and giving us the wine, which the sommelier had paired with our entrée. We look at each other and take the first bite of this course. We both moan our appreciation and laugh. We eat our entrée in shared silence, enjoying the flavors as they intermingle on our palates. When we are done, we push our plates to the side and watch the fountain outside.

The energy around us is peaceful but also filled with promise. I need to say the rest of what I started saying earlier. Slowly, I turn to him, and he turns to me. And I resume the conversation, "Delicious is not a word for a friend, but I might be okay with that." My voice comes out a little more seductive than intended. Interesting.

"Really?...... You mind telling me why?" His voice has dropped an octave, and his thumb is rubbing circles on the back of my hand that he has just re-picked up.

I watch his thumb's movement as I continue, "Well, see, the other thing that I realized, after talking it over with God in the oxygen room, is that I have been lying to myself for some time now. I made myself believe I could be ok without having the person I knew I wanted and needed.... I thought I could be happy falling in line with the vision of life that I had come up with, i.e., my own life vision. However, deep down, I knew that that vision was incomplete, at least for me. God gave me a choice today; I can have a part of what He is offering by starting this new business, or I can have all of what He is offering by choosing both the business and you." I look up into his eyes.

He does not move, and even his thumb has stopped moving. His eyes encouraged me to continue, but he said nothing; he just waited. I sigh, look at our hands, and start making circles with my thumb. Returning my gaze to his, I say, "I wasn't ready then, but I am now. I choose to have it all. I want the job that uses my gifts and brings me joy. I want the family with the man I adore. Most of all, I can finally be honest with myself. Most of all...... I want you." I take a moment and then say assuredly while gazing deeply into his dark brown eyes, "Monroe, Baby, I choose you."

Before I can say anything else, Roe has picked me up and has me sitting in his lap. He is running his thumb across my cheeks. I see him processing what I just said, but he hasn't said anything. I lean closer to him and do the one thing I have wanted to do all evening. I press my lips gently against his, kissing him softly until he places his fingers behind my neck and buries them in the nape of my hair. He tilts his head, and our kiss deepens. He tastes like our food and wine, and that wonderful flavor that is only him. I didn't realize how much I had been searching for the taste of him over the past five years. Now that I have it, I never want to let it go.

When we have no choice but to come up for air, we break our kiss and lean our foreheads against the other's. Breathing in each other's exhale, we finally lean back so we can gaze into one another's eyes.

Then, in that deep octave I love, he says, "LeShay, I choose you, too."

Part 3 - Forever and Always:

Epilogue

Chapter 16 - Monroe

Exactly **five months ago,** LeShay and I started dating. After that romantic dinner, we took a stroll and discussed our new divine life visions, what they entailed, and what we wanted. We decided to give us, as a couple, a chance, finally. Since then, a lot has changed. Shay is working on starting her business. She says she must have the right things in place before she starts. She moved into a townhouse close to my house. I expanded my gallery and am almost done with the fountain from my dream.

These are the things I am thinking about as I drive to meet Shay to look at yet another location for her business. She says she is looking for the perfect place, and I get that. But this will be the 10th place we have seen. I am not complaining; I am just saying. I pull into the blacktop parking lot at a medium-sized warehouse building. There are other parking spaces right in front of the building. The building looks freshly renovated, but still has that industrial charm that makes you think of an art district. I partially expect to see an art studio as I walk into Studio B, which is the studio suite she is looking at.

However, when I walked into the space, I knew it was the space we had been looking for. It has everything she wants, from high ceilings to movable walls to gorgeous oversized windows. In my mind's eye, I can see her drafting table and swatch-boarding stations already. There is a wall that would be perfect as an accent wall. As I stand there, I envision the perfect mural. It would be a mixture of black, purple, and turquoise, like her logo. There in the middle would be her company motto, which is "Loving is Living. Love the Space you Live in." Then, there would be a beautiful backdrop of a bouquet of white calla lilies in a crystal vase with a view of the ocean and the setting sun behind it.

I am so lost in this idea that I don't realize that Shay has walked in from one of the back rooms and is watching me from the door frame. Her realtor is standing behind her. When my eyes meet LeShay's, my heart melts. She looks beautiful in her long-sleeved maxi dress. Her locs are in a messy bun with a clip holding them in place. However, it is her eyes that do me in. Every time I look into them, I see love, clarity, and hope. I give her a wink.

"Hey, gorgeous," I say as I walk toward her.

"Hey, Baby." When I reach her, she wraps her arms around me and gives me a peck on the lips, then hugs me close.

After greeting my woman, I greet the realtor. The realtor asks if LeShay wants to give me a tour as the realtor takes a call. Shay says yes. However, instead of walking me to the back, she leads me back to the space I just vacated when I saw her watching me.

"Roe, what did you see?" She asks.

"A whole mural right here. When you get this place, please let me paint you one as an accent wall."

"When I get this place, huh? So, you think it is perfect?"

"Yeah, it has everything, and I haven't even seen the back rooms." I look at her, and she is expressionless. Did I miss something? She sees me eyeing her and then bursts out laughing.

Grinning at me, she says, "Relax, Bae. You are right. This place is perfect, and I would love for you to paint me a mural."

"Bae, huh?"

She leans into me, and I wrap my arms around her waist. "That's what you are, right, Roe? You are my best friend, my lover, and my man. You're definitely, Bae." She says that last part seductively alluring and sexy.

"Forever and Always, LeShay. Forever and always, I will be your Bae." With that, we share a long, all-consuming kiss. When we lean back, I gaze into her beautiful eyes and speak the words that have been etched in my heart and spirit over the last few weeks, "I'm in love with you, Bae."

She beams sweetly, taking hold of my heart even more, and speaks the truth written in her eyes, "I'm in love with you, too, Bae."

Sharing those words for the first time as a couple feels inspiring and freeing. We allow ourselves a few minutes to enjoy the present moment and to enjoy the feeling of wholeness and completeness surrounding us as we have finally owned the truth and destiny that we have to offer each other. I feel God's presence before I hear him say, "Well done."

After a few more minutes, we tour the rest of the space, which is indeed perfect. Shay is sure this is the spot. Therefore, we walk out to meet the realtor. I stand to the side as I watch Shay make her offer for the space. She waves me over to join their conversation. My heart swells with warmth and pride. The truth is, we have always given each other space to handle our business, but more recently, we have begun to include the other person in business decisions. This couple's dynamic between us is calming, loving, reassuring, and supportive. I feel like I can do anything as long as she is with me for the journey, and that is not a feeling I have ever had in any other intimate relationship.

After finishing with the realtor, we decided to walk down to the food truck park at the end of the street. As we walk in comfortable silence, I think about how much I love the woman next to me, how much I know that one day soon, I will ask her to be my wife, and we will begin our next phase together. Until then, I will continue to enjoy these moments we are having right now.

I look down and see her watching me. I wrap my arm around her as we continue our walk. I do not offer any words or explanations of my thoughts, and she does not push. We simply continue in the silence and enjoy the other person's company, space, and energy.

Who would have thought a dream could lead you in the direction of your true forever? Who would have thought it was possible for time to make you ready for the fulfillment of the dream, piece by piece and part by part? Who would have thought that time would be enough to prepare for the dream that has always been nearby? Who would have thought that a dream could lead you to divine life vision? Who would have thought.....

Now, I truly understand that, as much as I wanted us to be a couple five years ago, it was not the right time. However, now is the perfect time for us to be an us. We are both ready to take on the life we truly want and the life that was divinely designed for us as individuals and as a couple.

Chapter 17 – LeShay

Two months later

I find myself, once again, walking in the neighborhood with different colored doors. Eventually, I get to the house with the purple door with a slight shimmer. Opening the door, something is different in the house. I just stepped in and haven't seen anything, but the feel of the house is different. Walking into the house, there is still a high-ceilinged foyer with a beautiful crystal chandelier. The sunshine still lands on the chandelier just right, allowing the crystals to sparkle throughout the foyer.

However, now, the wall color is light gray in the opening of the foyer, and the foyer walls are not straight but in a diagonal that meets at the purple door behind me. There is also a new vase of purple and white calla lilies on an end table to my left. I set my keys and purse on the end of the table. It is then that I realize that I used my keys to open the purple door this time.

A mirror is hanging above the flowers, and when I glance at myself, I see that I glow. I have a lovely bronze shimmer to my chocolate skin, and my eyes dance with happiness. My locs are styled so that I appear to have a short pixie cut with beautiful purple, turquoise, and silver loc confetti. I look happy, like extremely, genuinely happy.

Then I noticed the painting behind me was of a man and a woman. In the painting, the man has a mocha skin tone, and the woman has a slightly lighter chocolate skin tone, just like me and Monroe. When I look to the bottom right, sure enough, it has M. Marquis T. in the corner, which is Monroe's artist signature.

I inhale the air, and it smells of vanilla and cedarwood, a wonderful blend that makes me realize exactly why this time in the house is different. This time, walking through the purple door, the house feels like home. I walk further into the living room and see that the space has been opened up. The layout is more efficient because the natural light of the large windows is allowed to brighten the rooms and provide a better view of the pool directly behind the house. Looking to the left of the pool, I see a garden that was not there before. I take in the living room furniture; it is no longer blue-gray but light gray, similar to the walls. The sofa has custom pillows with a blue and purple design. The rug on the floor beneath the glass coffee table has the same hues of blue and purple as the pillows.

As I continued to peruse the living room, I noticed a massive TV mounted above the white stone fireplace on the wall to my left. I can also see the surround sound speakers in the ceiling of the space. They are nicely hidden within the walls so that most people would miss them entirely. These, too, had to be customized. I turn to my right, and there is an open kitchen with deep gray cabinets and light gray and white marble countertops. The cabinets have designs along the bottom in the blue and purple hues from the living space. It makes the kitchen appear to be the accent wall and not just the kitchen; that concept is truly a great idea. The kitchen is complete with a bar and island topped with the same marble as the counters. On top of the island is another bouquet of purple and white calla lilies.

I feel a shift in the room's energy as I look toward the dining room. I know who caused this shift of energy without looking. It is my lover, my best friend, my man, my Monroe. I turn to see him and gaze into his eyes as he leans on the doorframe of the master bedroom. He beckons me to him with his finger, and my feet move of their own accord. When I reach him, he picks me up. My legs instantly wrap around him, and I am secure in his embrace.

He kisses me deeply and thoroughly, leaving no part of my mouth untouched by his tongue. I bask in the kiss that always makes me want more. He breaks the kiss and walks us into the master bedroom. This time, the master contains a deep, dark, midnight blue accent wall with a light gray high-back sparkling headboard. Before I take in the rest of the room, I am thrown on the custom mattress that hugs me instantly. Monroe stands in front of me as I sit up on my elbows, and I can see the garden behind him since this room has a bay window, and the center window is a floor-to-ceiling folding glass patio door. Monroe grins down at me and says, "Welcome home, Bae."

I must look at him, confused, because he smirks. Then he leans on his arms in front of me and says, "It is time to come home, Bae. Wake up."

With that, my eyes open, and I beam into myself. It's time to come home; what does that mean? I hear my phone beep, alerting me to a text. I reach out to my phone lying on my coffee table as I napped on the sofa before dinner with Monroe. Looking at my phone, I see that it's Roe texting.

Hey Bae, change of plans. We r eatin in tonite at my house.

Ur house? Oh, I finally get to see Chateau Thibodeaux?

Y u sound all feisty?

U know it is weird that I have not been to your house this whole time right?

True

If I didn't know u I would think u had a whole wife and kids u didn't want me to know about

But you do know me and u know that u are the only one I want to be my wife and have my kids

Uhm. Don't be tryin to sweet talk me, Roe.

I see the three dots blink, and I wait for his response. I love messing with him. I can't help it. However, I get confused when I do not see a message, and the blinking stops. What happened? A few minutes passed, and still no response was sent. I text.

Roe?

I wait a few more minutes. Shoot, I pressed a nerve. I was just kidding. See, that is the problem with texting. Things get lost in translation.

I put on my shoes to go apologize, and then I remembered that I did not actually know his address. Shoot. I was not kidding when I said I had not been to his house. Literally, we have been dating for seven months, and I have not been to my man's house. My friends think it's sus, and I would too if I didn't know Monroe. But I do know him, and he doesn't invite people to his house until it is completely decorated. It's his thing. I think now that he is entirely into his artist's side, it's worse than before. He needs everything to be in its proper place and fully decorated with all the details having been tended to. Then, and only then, are guests allowed in his home, including me. The closest I have gotten to anything pertaining to his house is color swatches. The same was true when he bought his first condo.

I looked at my text messages again, and still no response. Shoot.

Roe, I was kiddin. Bae you know I was.

I wait, but still nothing. Before I can call him to clear things up, there is a knock at my door. It is probably my neighbor coming to get the wine we discussed earlier. When I open the door, there is a shift in the energy, and I am met with Roe's handsome, slightly irritated face.

"Oh, you better have been kiddin." He leans in and kisses me softly. He walks us into my townhouse and then shuts the door. He backs me up into the wall by the door.

"Roe, I was kiddin."

"It didn't sound like it."

"You could have just called."

"You could have put an emoji with those words."

"Fair. I'm sorry."

"Thank you."

"So, you came here to what? Punish me?" I smile.

He shakes his head with a smile, "I can do that... But no."

"Then what?"

"Prove my point." He steps back and drops to one knee. "LeShay, Baby.... Bae," He grins. "I love you more than I ever thought someone could love another. You make me happy. You bring me excitement and joyful peace. I am happy that we took the time to turn into an us, and now I want us forever and always. So, LeShay Michelle Fontenot, will you marry me?"

With tears in my eyes and loving peace in my heart, I say, "Yes, Roe, I will."

It is then that he takes out a two-carat marquis diamond set in platinum and puts it on my left ring finger. He stands up and kisses me thoroughly, like he did in my dream. Umm. So good.

"Shay, you said yes without a diamond."

"Bae, I knew you would come up with one at some point. Plus, it's you I want."

"Good because, like I said, you are the only wife I want and the only woman that I want to have my kids."

After another toe-curling kiss, he takes me to his car, and we head to his house. His house is in a gated community. It is actually really close to my townhouse. A fact that he did not share when I purchased my townhouse. Interesting. As we turned down his street, I noticed his neighbors had front doors with different colors.

My breath catches in my chest. I struggle to breathe as we pass different houses with various colored doors. I whisper, "Roe?"

"Just wait, Bae. Breathe." He says calmly, and he squeezes my hand. I slow my breathing to almost normal, and then he pulls up to the front of a house with a purple door. It's *the house* and *the purple door*. I look at him with tears in my eyes. He gets out of the car and comes to open my door. He takes my hand and leads me up the walkway, just like in my first dream about this house.

When we walk in, everything looks like the dream I just had during my nap, from the chandelier in the foyer to the calla lilies to the custom pillows on the sofa with blue and purple designs to the kitchen. He grabs my hand and takes me to the back of the house.

In the back of the house, we pass the pool from my dreams and walk into the garden. The garden I just dreamt about, but did not get to see completely. We walk through the garden, taking in the white lilies that I love and roses that are beautiful shades of red and purple. When we get to the end of the garden, it is then that I realize the garden is V-shaped, and at the apex is a gorgeous fountain lit up with lights. The fountain is of a woman and a man intertwined in a lover's intimate embrace.

"LeShay, I intended for us to have dinner, and then I was going to bring you out here and ask you for your hand in marriage. I wanted to show you that the house we have dreamt about all these years is real, just like my love for you always has been."

I throw my arms around him. "You built our house, Roe? You live here... in our dream?"

"Yeah, I do. It's time for you to come home, Bae."

"Yes, it is. I love you, Bae."

As we lean in for a kiss, we say in unison, "Forever and Always."

The End.

Author's Note

Thank you for taking this journey of *Dreaming of You* with me. It is wild to know that sometimes God chooses to talk to us in our dreams. It is also comforting to know that all we really have to do is follow the Creator's leading, and we will reach the divine life visions for our lives. Life has ups and downs, but when we follow God, things truly work out for our good. Once again, thank you for taking this journey with me. Please look out for my next book, *Losing You*. As you wait, please read some of my other books on Amazon or www.peacebeloved.co. You can also reach out to me via email at beloved@peacebeloved.co. Without you, I could not do what I love. I appreciate your support. I wish you all the love and joyful peace. Let's walk our divine life visions! Peace Beloved, Minniel

Novels by Minniel Douglas

(All Titles are available on Amazon/Kindle)

Nonfiction:

The 7 Principles for Manifesting in Abundance

Fiction:

Poweress Series:

Power of Finding You

Power of Truth

Power of Honesty

Power of Acceptance